"I'm ⟨barcode⟩ too."

Kathr⟨barcode: D0012903⟩ uch, but he pulled

"Not yet. I need this first."

In a lightning quick move, his mouth closed over hers. The hunger of it caused her to gasp. He didn't pretend to coax a response from her. His blatant longing was unmistakable. They were crossing a line here where fun had been left behind and the real stuff of life was happening.

To deny him now could cause permanent damage. She didn't *want* to deny him anything, but it meant exposing the heart she'd been guarding for years.

"Colt—" she cried, before she gave up the battle and began kissing him back with a passion she hadn't known herself capable of.

Dear Reader,

Four years ago I wrote a two-book miniseries for Harlequin Superromance called Lost & Found: *Somebody's Daughter* (#1259) and *The Daughter's Return* (#1282). Both books are still available on www.Amazon.com.

These novels came about because of my interest in the Elizabeth Smart kidnapping case that caught the attention of our whole nation. I live five minutes from the Smart home in Salt Lake City, Utah, and actively grieved and prayed for that family. One of my good friends and her husband flew their private plane over the hillsides, looking for Elizabeth. My children tied yellow ribbons to the school fencing, exhibiting their hope for her safe return. It was a terrible time that left a deep scar on our city, state and country. When Elizabeth turned up alive nine months later, the rejoicing over this miracle was heard far and wide. I can't tell you how happy I was for her and her family.

That joy translated into my writing a story about a woman who was kidnapped and eventually made it back home. It took two books to get the whole story down. Since then, I've received mail from loyal readers wanting to know what happened to my character Kathryn McFarland after she was returned to her family. Did she end up with Steve, a handsome attorney?

You'll find out the answer when you read *Santa in a Stetson*. Kathryn has been home four years.

Enjoy!

Rebecca Winters

Santa in a Stetson
REBECCA WINTERS

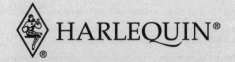

HARLEQUIN®

TORONTO • NEW YORK • LONDON
AMSTERDAM • PARIS • SYDNEY • HAMBURG
STOCKHOLM • ATHENS • TOKYO • MILAN • MADRID
PRAGUE • WARSAW • BUDAPEST • AUCKLAND

Recycling programs
for this product may
not exist in your area.

ISBN-13: 978-0-373-75335-2

SANTA IN A STETSON

Copyright © 2010 by Rebecca Winters

Printed in U.S.A.

ABOUT THE AUTHOR

Rebecca Winters, whose family of four children has now swelled to include five beautiful grandchildren, lives in Salt Lake City, Utah, in the land of the Rocky Mountains. With canyons and high alpine meadows full of wildflowers, she never runs out of places to explore. They, plus her favorite vacation spots in Europe, often end up as backgrounds for her romance novels, because writing is her passion, along with her family and church. Rebecca loves to hear from readers. If you wish to email her, please visit her website at www.cleanromances.com.

Books by Rebecca Winters

HARLEQUIN AMERICAN ROMANCE

HARLEQUIN SUPERROMANCE

HARLEQUIN ROMANCE

Dedicated to the Smart family, who never gave up or lost hope. You and your courageous daughter are an exemplary model in faith for the rest of us.

Chapter One

"The bus is coming. Bye, Dad. Don't forget I'm going to Jen's house after school for a sleepover. Her mom is driving us all home tomorrow so you won't have to worry about it." Allie leaned across the front seat of the truck and gave him a hug.

"I haven't forgotten anything, but I think your cold's worse," Colton Brenner said. Throughout the week, her congestion had become more noticeable. "Maybe you'd better give this party a miss and have an early night."

"I can't! It would ruin the whole weekend!" She sounded so upset he was sorry he'd said anything. "We've made too many plans, but I promise not to stay up late. The decongestant pills you gave me are in my purse."

"If you're not improved tomorrow, I'm taking you to the doctor."

"Everyone has a cold right now. It's not a big deal." Her warm brown eyes slid away from his. When they did that, it signaled she didn't want to get into a heavy discussion with him.

"But not everyone is *my* daughter." He kissed her cheek. "I love my children."

"We love you, too." She opened the door and got out.

"Later!" his son called from the backseat.

He turned. "Bye, Matt. I'll be at your wrestling match at three o'clock."

"Don't forget it's in Livingston."

"Would I do that?" They high-fived each other before he jumped down. "We'll go for pizza after."

"Cool!" Matt shut the door.

Colton—Colt to his friends—sat back in the seat, eyeing his fifteen-year-old twins as they waited for the school bus that would drive them into Bozeman eight miles away.

Every morning he brought them down to the entrance of the Circle B to make sure they got off safely. The family always ate breakfast together and talked over the day's plans. His housekeeper Noreen picked them up at the same spot after school. It was a ritual he'd started years earlier and had never deviated from.

When their mother had pulled her permanent disappearing act, he'd made it his mission to be there for them in every possible capacity. He loved them more than life.

This morning their breath curled in the invigorating air. Twenty degrees above zero wasn't bad for mid-November in the Bridger Mountains of Montana. He could remember other Novembers at twenty below. Unfortunately the weather couldn't be good for Allie's cold.

More snow wasn't forecast until tomorrow evening. With a lull between storms, this was the best time for him and his foreman to ride up to the north forty with some of the hands and finish repairs on the fencing. If he left with them now, he'd be able to get in a good six hours of work before he had to leave for Livingston, twenty-six miles away.

Now that football season was over and Matt's team had lost in the playoffs, Matt had joined the wrestling squad. His school's first preseason match was today. The boy was shooting up, but he wanted to get more buff. Colt smiled. He remembered wanting the same thing at Matt's age.

After his children boarded the bus, he waved to the driver before heading back to the ranch house three miles up the mountain. His eyes took in the blanket of snow covering evergreen forests and copses of aspens. He loved it all, from harshest winter to the glory of summer, when wildflowers filled the alpine meadows. Every season highlighted different aspects of the ranch's beauty and brought him renewal.

Thanks to his Scottish ancestors who'd emigrated here in the late 1800s, the setting of the Brenner cattle ranch was the most beautiful mountain spread this side of the Continental Divide. He counted his blessings.

The one thing missing from his life hadn't mattered to him in years. He'd long since put the pain of his travesty of a marriage behind him. Though everything else had failed during those nightmarish twelve months of supposed wedded bliss, he and his nineteen-year-old bride had made perfect babies together. Matthew and Allison…nonidentical brunettes who came with their own individual spirits.

Loving his children, working the ranch to leave them a legacy for the future, was his reason for living.

THIRTY-YEAR-OLD Kathryn McFarland had the distinction of having been kidnapped from her parents' mansion on South Temple in Salt Lake City, Utah, and lost to them for the first twenty-six years of her life. The people at Skwars Farm, Wisconsin, who'd taken her in had called her Anna Buric. Her origins were a mystery to everyone. Then one day a miracle happened.

She was found!

In an instant, she'd become Kathryn McFarland. And like the pauper who'd suddenly been thrust on the throne as the Prince of England, she inherited lands, titles, wealth and a loving, illustrious family eager to embrace her.

That was more than four years ago. Yet every time she let herself inside her penthouse condo at the McFarland Plaza in downtown Salt Lake, she experienced alternating waves of gratitude and guilt—gratitude because she'd been united with the most wonderful, generous parents imaginable and guilt because she needed her own space.

She knew it seemed unfair to her family that after waiting twenty-six years to get their little baby back, Kathryn had returned a grown woman who needed her family desperately, but secretly needed her independence, too.

They'd lost all that time with each other. So had she, with them. It was only natural for her to live with them and bask in their love, but it couldn't go on forever.

Kit Talbot McFarland, Kathryn's sister-in-law, knew exactly how Kathryn felt. She, too, had been kidnapped as a baby in the same bizarre case twenty-six years earlier, and had been found a few months before Kathryn.

But in the process she'd met Cord, one of Kathryn's two older brothers. It wasn't long before they were married and now had a little girl and another baby on the way.

From the beginning Kathryn shared a unique bond with Kit. She, too, suffered untold guilt for not spending more time with her birth parents and family, who lived in California. Kit and Kathryn were painfully aware that both sets of parents, the McFarlands and the Talbots, had suffered "empty arms syndrome" for more than two decades.

To some degree, Kit's two-year-old daughter helped satisfy that ache in the Talbots' lives, but Kathryn had no husband or children. She wasn't even close to starting her own family. Which was why Kathryn's parents couldn't understand why she wouldn't continue to live with them in their home in Federal Heights, only a few miles from the plaza.

They didn't outwardly pressure her. It was more the pleading in their eyes, the unspoken message, hinting they wanted her with them. All those silent hopes played havoc with Kathryn's guilt.

Thank heaven for Maggie!

There weren't enough words to describe Kathryn's love for her older sister Maggie McFarland, the mother of a one-year-old boy. She, along with her husband, Jake Halsey, had been the ones to find Kathryn in Wisconsin and bring her home.

Soon after their family reunion had made headlines in every newspaper in the nation, Maggie and Jake married and built a house in upper Federal Heights. When they were settled, Maggie insisted Kathryn move into the penthouse where Maggie had been living in order to have some breathing room.

Their mother's fear of another kidnapping had made her so overprotective, she'd almost suffocated Maggie at times growing up. Now that Kathryn was finally home, Maggie could see the same thing happening to her sister and told her she needed to get out of the house and on her own.

"There needs to be spaces in your togetherness," she'd whispered to Kathryn at her wedding.

"Listen to Maggie," their oldest married brother Ben concurred in a low voice. "She knows what she's talking about."

Cord nodded. "We've all lived with horrific guilt for twenty-six years because no one heard the kidnapper come into the house and steal you away. Now that you've been found alive and are home again, everyone needs to get on with their lives. No more guilt. No more looking back."

With those words, Kathryn understood her siblings were her best friends and allies. Between them, they took care of the move and got her settled on top of the McFarland Tower. Every window looked out on a superb view of the Salt Lake Valley and the mountains encircling it.

From the kitchen, she had an eastern exposure and could see Mount Olympus, covered in snow. This morning while she'd been working with Cord, he'd told her there was fresh powder up Little Cottonwood Canyon in Alta, where he and Kit lived.

They'd made plans to ski tomorrow. Their first outing of the season. She couldn't wait. Cord was a fabulous skier and had given her lessons every winter. Kathryn was getting pretty good at it, if she said so herself.

Cord was the true mountain man of the family. In that regard, they were soul mates—like the first McFarland who'd claimed a lot of land in the Albion Basin for his own before the turn of the last century.

She'd seen it for the first time in summer, when the meadows were a riot of wildflowers. A euphoric Kathryn had thought she loved that season best until fall arrived and the trees turned to gold and flame everywhere she hiked.

Then came the majesty of winter, so white and gorgeous. She hated to see it go, but when spring followed and the primroses poked their pink heads out of the melting snow, the signs of new life filled her with indescribable yearnings for the changes yet to come. After living in a flat part of the country so many years, she couldn't get enough of the Rockies and was a constant visitor to Cord's mountain home.

When she heard her iPhone ring, she'd just taken a bite of peach yogurt. It was probably her brother making final arrangements for tomorrow. She clicked on and said hello.

"Hi, Kathryn. It's Bonnie Frank." The woman worked at North Avenues Hospital in the patient advocacy department funded by the McFarland Foundation.

"Hey, Bonnie. How are you?"

"Ask me tomorrow morning when I haven't been on my feet all day."

Kathryn chuckled. "I hear you." She took some more bites. "What's going on?"

"The E.R. just contacted me. A teenage runaway was

admitted a few minutes ago after collapsing on a downtown street. Nancy Isom was the head nurse on duty and she couldn't get any information from the girl, so she called my office asking for you. I know it's dinnertime, but do you think you could drop by the hospital sometime this evening and interview this one? I've gotten absolutely nowhere with her."

"I'll come now." The sooner she dealt with the problem, the sooner she could get to bed. A day of skiing gave her a real workout and needed to be fortified with a good night's sleep.

"You're an angel. I'll let them know you're on your way."

Kathryn rang off before freshening up in the bathroom. After making sure she had a McFarland Foundation brochure in her purse, she put on her parka and left the condo.

The private elevator took her to the underground car park where the security guard waved to her. She got in her Jeep and took off for the hospital, located a mile away. She phoned her parents en route to see how their day had gone.

After all those years, when she'd wondered if she had a mother and father who were even alive, it seemed miraculous that Kathryn could call them up whenever she felt like it. She adored them.

THERE WAS ONE SLICE of pizza left in the pan. Colt glanced at Matt. "Do you want to wrestle for the last piece?"

He screwed up his face. "That's all right, Dad. I want to live to see another day. You can have it."

Colt laughed. "I liked that reversal you came up with before the ref blew the whistle. Good job."

"Thanks." Matt reached for the pizza, as Colt knew he would, and made short work of it.

The waitress came to refill their glasses, but Colt shook his head. After she walked away, he pulled out his wallet and left a couple of bills on the table. "Shall we?"

They both got to their feet at the same time and shrugged into their parkas before heading for the entrance to the pizza parlor. "Hey, Dad, want to see a movie?"

"Sure. With your sister gone, we'll make it an official guys' night out." They walked into the frigid air. "What's playing?"

"The latest vampire film."

"I thought that was a chick flick," he teased.

"It is, but Marcus was talking about it at the match. He said it was pretty good."

"I guess I can stand it if you can. Allie can't seem to get enough of the *Twilight* series."

Two hours later Colt said, "Believe it or not, I liked it."

"Me, too!" Matt blurted, eager to talk about it as they left the theater.

Halfway to the truck, parked around the corner, they heard, "Hi, Matt! Hi, Mr. Brenner! Where's Allie?"

He glanced around, surprised to see Carrie and Michelle, two of Allie's good friends. Colt would have thought they'd be at the sleepover, but evidently they hadn't been invited. Allie had given him the impression it would be a big group. It appeared somebody must have hurt somebody else's feelings. Diplomacy was called for.

"She made other plans. Did you two like the film?"

Michelle smiled. "We loved it."

"Did *you?*" Carrie asked Matt.

"It was okay," he answered in a quiet voice, hiding his enthusiasm.

Colt got a kick out of his son, who acted like a typical male around girls. At that age, shyness hadn't been one of Colt's problems. His ease around girls had probably facilitated his early marriage. Would that Matt took a little longer to grow up before he made a commitment that would change his life.

They reached the corner. "See you girls later. Don't let any vampires bite you tonight."

The girls broke into laughter. "Bye, Mr. Brenner."

"Bye, Matt." Carrie again.

His son said something indistinct before they parted company and headed for the truck.

On the way home he turned to Matt. "This morning on the bus, did your sister say anything about a quarrel with her friends?"

"No." He darted him a curious glance. "Why do you ask?"

"Because I thought all Allie's friends were going to be over at Jen's tonight."

Matt shrugged. "I don't know, but she was kind of quiet on the bus."

Her cold could account for that, but Colt still wasn't reassured. An uneasiness had crept over him he couldn't explain, but she'd hate it if he phoned her at Jen's. No teenager liked to be checked up on at a party.

He rubbed his jaw where he could feel the beginnings of a beard. "I guess we'll find out tomorrow after she gets home."

"Dad?"

Did Matt know something after all? "Yes?"

"I think something's wrong with Blackie's hind leg."

"He needs reshoeing," Colt murmured, his mind still on his daughter. "In the morning we'll get it taken care of before we load up more hay to take to the west pasture." He drove up to the side of the ranch house and turned off the motor.

"After that, is it okay if I go skiing with Rich? We'll buy a half-day pass."

"Sounds fun."

They both got out and walked around to the back. "You want to come with us?"

"I'd like to, but Noreen says the kitchen disposal is having problems. Since Ed's arm is still in a cast, I promised I'd take a look at it. If it needs to be replaced, that could take some time." For a variety of reasons, Colt wanted to be on hand when Allie got dropped off. "Let's go skiing next Saturday. Maybe Rich's dad will want to come, too."

"I'll ask him."

"Sounds like a plan." Colt followed him to the back porch. They stomped the snow off their cowboy boots before entering the house. Ten minutes later they both said good-night.

Colt checked with Noreen, who lived in the older

house on the property with her husband, Ed, Colt's ranch manager. Noreen hadn't heard from Allie. Not that he expected her to call, but when he entered his study, he knew he wouldn't sleep until he'd talked to his daughter.

Without hesitation, he called her cell phone. Her voice mail came on. He asked her to call him back when she could, then rang off.

Frustrated when another twenty minutes passed with no response, he looked up the Wagners' number in the phone directory. Even though it was ten-thirty, he called them, but their voice mail came on, too. He left the message that he'd like Allie to call her father, then he hung up.

Maybe the Wagners had taken the girls to a movie or ice skating. The thought that they were all out together should have relieved him. Colt was probably obsessing for nothing, and yet...

His thoughts flew back ten years to the time when he'd gotten a strange foreboding about his grandmother. It had been early morning. Though he'd just arrived in the upper pasture with some of the hands, he turned right around and galloped home to discover his grandfather weeping over her body. "Her heart stopped beating a half hour ago, Colton. She's gone."

Unnerved by the memory, he decided he couldn't sit around waiting for the phone to ring. He hurried down the hall and took the stairs two at a time to Matt's room. His son was listening to his iPod.

When he saw him, he sat up in bed with a jerk. "Dad?"

"Get dressed and come with me to Jen's house."

"What's wrong?"

"Maybe nothing. I just need to make sure Allie's all right."

"Okay." He slid out of bed to put on his clothes.

"I'll meet you at the truck."

ON HER WAY INTO THE E.R., Kathryn glanced around the lounge filled with friends and relatives of the patients. The place had never looked busier. She approached the desk and spotted Nancy, who was simultaneously talking on the phone while she entered information on the computer. The two women had become friends while Kathryn was getting her RN degree.

As soon as she saw Kathryn, she flashed a smile of relief and hung up. "Thanks for coming so fast. Our uncommunicative runaway is down the hall in the isolation area, Room Six. Her tests just came back. She's got the H1N1 virus."

"Is she coherent?"

"Oh, yes, but she won't tell us how long she's had symptoms. I think she's been sick for a while. When they wheeled her in, she was very upset about being brought to the hospital. She told us to let her go. If she's refusing to talk, it's because she's terrified about something. When the ambulance picked her up, she had no ID on her."

"Where was she found?"

"Down near the Rio Grande Café. A pedestrian saw her collapse and called 911."

One of the homeless shelters was near there. The airport, the Greyhound bus depot and the Amtrak station were all close by, and it seemed possible she'd come in from out of town.

"Did she speak with an accent? You know—Alabama, Boston, Texas, New *Joysey?*"

Nancy laughed at her imitation and thought for a minute. "Nothing stood out. I'd say she's from somewhere in the western states, but no central Utah drawl if you know what I mean." They both smiled.

Good. That narrowed the field a little. "You want me to tell her about her condition?"

"Yes. I'm hoping that when you do, she'll break down and open up to you. See what you can get out of her, will you?"

"Sure."

Kathryn went around to a back room where she shed her parka. After removing the brochure from her purse, she stowed everything in a locker, then washed her hands. Donning a surgical mask and lab coat, she then slipped a small notepad and pen in her pocket along with the brochure and found her way down several halls to Room Six.

They'd hooked up an IV to the pretty brunette lying there in a hospital gown with her eyes closed. Before she did anything else, Kathryn opened the girl's locker and took her bag of clothes out in the hall to examine.

She'd been wearing a North Face parka, navy jeans, a red, long-sleeved pullover sweater, Nike Air Morgans with hook-and-ladder fasteners, and tube socks. Everything higher end and clean. No smell of smoke. All items could have been purchased in a major department store anywhere across the nation.

After Kathryn returned the bag back to the locker,

she walked over to the computer and brought up the police report first.

> Jane Doe. Age 14–16. Caucasian. Picked up at 4:10 p.m., Friday, Nov 19. A pedestrian, Ronald Ewing, 50, Grantsville, Utah, saw her slump onto the sidewalk at 300 south, fifth west, Salt Lake, and called emergency on his cell phone. Approx height 5´5˝, weight 115 pounds, brown hair, brown eyes, teeth in excellent condition. No evidence of alcohol. No needle marks. No sign of drugs hidden on her body or in her clothes. No purse or wallet. No money. No injury marks, no sign of assault, rape or foul play.

There were a lot more things Kathryn could add simply by looking at her. Aside from the fact that she had the flu, she was the picture of health and excellent hygiene. Her nails were well cared for, her shoulder-length hair had a gloss to it.

The hospital stats indicated a fever of 101.4 when she was brought in. No vomiting or diarrhea. They were hydrating her and giving her medicine to bring down her temperature. Since the last check of vital signs, there'd been a drop of one degree. That was good news.

She was someone's darling.

Kathryn snagged a stool and sat down at the side of the hospital bed. "Hi, Anna. I'm Katy."

The girl opened her eyes. They were velvety brown. Lovely eyes. Anxious.

"Don't let the mask scare you. It's a protective measure because you're fighting the H1N1 virus, but judging by the progress you're already making, it's not such a serious case. Unless I made a lucky guess, I know your name isn't Anna. I gave you *my* old name. The one I was given after I was kidnapped. It's as good as any."

Anna blinked. If Kathryn didn't miss her guess, she'd gained the girl's attention.

"I brought a brochure with me. My family had it printed when I was taken from them." She pulled it out of her purse. "Let me show you the picture of me at the top." Kathryn held it up so she could see it. With her other hand, she pulled down the mask so the girl could see they were one in the same person. Then she put it back in place.

"It was taken four years ago. You'll notice what it says beneath the picture. 'Kathryn McFarland, lost for twenty-six years, has been FOUND!' You're probably feeling too tired to read it, Anna, so I'll read it to you." Kathryn continued to read.

May 3 marks the twenty-sixth anniversary of the abduction of our fourth child, Kathryn Mc-Farland, from the McFarland home in Salt Lake City, Utah. Born April 2, she was only a month old at the time she was taken.

Soon after the kidnapping and community search, the Kathryn McFarland Foundation was founded and now honors Kathryn's memory by finding missing children, and preventing them from going missing in the first place.

When Kathryn was kidnapped, our community and many others joined together to help us find her because there was an immediate recognition that she was everyone's child and that we are all in this together.

Child abductions across our nation since its beginning have highlighted the need for legislation to enhance our ability to protect our children from predators of all types. When a child is kidnapped, time is of the essence.

All too often it is only a matter of hours before a kidnapper commits an act of violence against the child. That is why we're pleased that the U.S. Senate has acted to pass legislation creating a national AMBER Alert system, which galvanizes entire communities to assist law enforcement in the timely search and safe return of child victims.

Since its inception, the foundation has assisted approximately seventeen thousand families and law enforcement agencies in their searches. We have seen over eight-five percent of those children returned home safely. This is what continues to give us hope.

Kathryn put the brochure down on the bedside table. "Someone out there—*somewhere*—is dying inside because you're missing, Anna. I don't know how long you've been missing, or why. I don't know if you were kidnapped and let go, or if you left home of your own free will.

"What I *do* know is that a beautiful young woman like you is very lucky not to have been exposed to serious danger. I also know that anyone who loves you is in agony right now, fearing the worst."

The girl's eyelids fluttered closed, but they couldn't hold back the trickle of tears.

"My family went through so much agony, they would have died if they hadn't decided to do something positive with their pain. Did you hear those statistics? Seventeen thousand families assisted. That figure has changed since four years ago. It's now twenty-three thousand, with an eighty-five percent rate of success.

"I have parents, two brothers and a sister who've dedicated their lives to helping children unite with their loved ones. Now that I've been found, I've devoted my life to helping someone like you get the help you need.

"Consider me a friend who's going to make certain you get well and are safe. My brother runs Renaissance House, a shelter for homeless women to assist them in getting reestablished. It's only a mile from here. After you're released from the hospital, I'll take you there. You'll like it. The big, beautiful mansion was my home before I was kidnapped. After that, my family moved. They couldn't bear the pain of living in a place where I had been stolen right out of the nursery during the night. Since that time, my brother turned it into a halfway house. He did it because he hoped that one day *I* might walk in."

Suddenly the girl broke down crying. Kathryn stood up to lean over her and smooth the hair from her temples. "I didn't tell you all this to make you cry. I just wanted you to know that you're not alone. Sleep now, Anna. I'll stay right here and take care of you. I'm a nurse who did my training in this hospital. You're among friends here."

After a long silence, "My name's Allie."

Joy.

"I like that name much better." She handed her some tissues. "Go ahead and blow your nose, Allie. You must have been congested for a few days now."

The teen nodded and blew hard. Kathryn handed her a receptacle. "I'm going to get you a cold drink. Fruit punch, Sprite, root beer, Coke, you name it."

"Fruit punch, please."

She had manners, too. "Coming right up."

Kathryn hurried down the hall to the desk. She pulled her mask down again. "Her name's Allie. She wants some fruit punch."

A beaming Nancy lifted her head. "I knew it! You have the magic touch. Be back in a tick."

In another minute, she returned with two cans. Kathryn thanked her and joined Allie, who'd reached for the brochure on the side table and was reading it.

"I'll raise your head so you can drink without choking. Say when."

Before long Allie had drained her drink. Kathryn took the empty can from her. "Better?"

"Yes, thank you."

"Shall I lower your head now?"

"Not yet. Where did that kidnapper take you?"

Kathryn sat down on the stool once more. "New York, then Wisconsin."

Allie's red-rimmed eyes studied her in fascination. "How did you find your parents?"

"I didn't. My sister and the man she's married to now found *me*. When my family came into my hospital room to see me for the first time, we all looked so much alike there was no question I belonged to them."

She blew her nose again. "You were in a hospital, too?"

"Yes. I'd been in a car accident and had broken my leg. Because of my cast, everyone had to be very careful when they hugged me, especially my dad. To this day, I don't know which one of us squeezed harder."

"My dad can squeeze hard."

"That's one of the great things about having a father. It still makes me cry to think how many years I lived without my parents." Kathryn's throat swelled with emotion. "I love mine so much, you can't imagine. My dad's incredible."

"So's mine. That's why—" She suddenly stopped talking and tears gushed from her eyes.

Unable to stay seated after realizing how upset the teen was, Kathryn stood up and clasped Allie's free hand. "The longer I live, the more I realize that none of us is exempt from pain." She handed her more tissue. "How long have you been sick, Allie?"

"I've had a cold all week. After I left the bus station I started to look for a taxi, but then this man on a bike grabbed my purse and rode away. It had all my money in it. That's when I got dizzy and fell down. Then another man walked by. He saw me and called the police. I begged him not to because then Dad would find out."

She grabbed hold of Kathryn's arm, staring at her with imploring eyes. "Dad doesn't know I came here. He thought I was at a sleepover. I planned to be back home by tomorrow so he would never find out. He *can't* find out!"

"Why not?"

"If he knew the reason, it would hurt him too much."

Oh, darling girl…

Chapter Two

Not two seconds after Colt parked in front of the Wagners' house, their car pulled into the driveway. Reed was with his wife. No one else was in the car.

Colt got out and walked over to them. Wendie rushed toward him. "It's good to see you." She gave him a hug and said hello to Matt, who'd trailed him.

"Hey, Colt." Reed broke out in a broad smile. "To what do we owe this honor?"

"Matt and I just got out of a movie and thought we'd come by to see how the sleepover's going before we drive home. Allie had a bad cold when she left for school. I almost didn't let her go and wanted to see if it was worse."

Both of them looked surprised. "What sleepover?" Wendie asked.

The question was like a punch to the gut. "Obviously there wasn't one. I thought something was wrong when I saw Michelle and Carrie at the movie. Did Allie come home with Jen after school?"

"No. I picked her up and took her to the orthodontist. Tonight she's been tending Chelsey and David so we could go to a wedding."

An icy sensation crept through Colt's veins.

"You haven't seen her since she left for school this morning?" she asked.

"No."

Matt shot him a worried glance.

"Come into the house," Reed urged. "We'll find out from Jen where she is."

The four of them went inside. Reed called to his blonde daughter, who came into the living room dressed in army fatigue pajamas. The second she saw Colt, she froze.

"Hi, Mr. Brenner." She didn't look in the least happy to see him. It was very unlike her.

"Pumpkin?" her father inserted. "Do you know where Allie is? She didn't come home from school today."

Jen averted her eyes so fast that it reminded Colt of his daughter when she'd told him her cold wasn't a big deal and she didn't want to talk about it.

Wendie put an arm around her. "If you have an idea where she is, tell Colt so we won't have to phone everyone we know. It's late. We'd hate to have to disturb people who might be in bed by now."

Jen kept her head bowed. "She made me promise not to tell."

"Tell what?" Colt asked, trying to remain calm.

"Yesterday she told me she wouldn't be at school today. She said she'd be back the next day and asked me to do her a favor, so I did."

"What favor?"

"When our homeroom teacher took roll this morning, I—I told her Allie was in the restroom and would come in with a late pass," she stammered. "That's why the school didn't call you."

"Jennifer Wagner!" Reed exploded.

"I know that was wrong, Dad. I'm sorry, Mr. Brenner. Allie said that in case you called here, I should get Chelsey to tell you all the girls had gone to a movie. But Allie was positive you wouldn't phone." Her voice wobbled, producing another moan from her parents.

Colt's body shuddered in reaction. "You have no idea where she went?"

"No. I'm really sorry. I shouldn't have agreed to help her." She started crying.

"It's not your fault, Jen. My daughter put you in an impossible position. For that *I'm* sorry."

Matt's stricken expression set off another alarm bell. "Maybe you should call the Greyhound bus depot and find out if she got on a bus this morning."

For his son to tell him that… "What do *you* know about this?"

His gaze didn't flinch. "Nothing, but last week when Rich and I went to the Bozeman Bowl after school, I thought I saw her going in the bus depot. Rich said I was just seeing things because a lot of girls wore North Face parkas. That night I asked her about it. She said she hadn't been downtown, but she got mad about it. I thought that was kind of weird for her to be upset about a simple question."

Colt whipped out his phone to call information. The minute he was connected to the depot, he told the person who answered to put him on with the manager. "This is an emergency."

"Just a moment, sir."

He felt as if someone had just sucked all the air out of his lungs.

"This is Mr. Padakis, the manager. How can I help you, Mr. Brenner?"

"My daughter's been missing since seven this morning. I thought she went to school, but I now believe she may have taken a bus today, probably this morning. Her name is Allison Brenner. She's fifteen. Before I call the police, can you find out if she purchased a ticket? Any information you can give me would be helpful."

"I'm sorry to hear this. Give me a moment. I'm looking in the system now. Yes, here she is. A. Brenner, Circle B Ranch. She bought a round-trip ticket to Salt Lake City."

Salt Lake? Allie didn't know anyone there. They had no family there.

"The bus left at 7:40 a.m. She's due back tomorrow at 5:00 p.m."

He gripped the phone tighter. "What time does that bus start back to Bozeman?"

"Let's see. 8:30 a.m."

That made it an eight-and-a-half hour trip. He checked his watch. She would have arrived in Salt Lake by four today. It gave her fifteen, sixteen hours to do whatever she planned to do in that amount of time. The stone in Colt's throat made it nearly impossible to talk.

"Thank you very much, Mr. Padakis."

"I hope everything's all right."

"So do I," he whispered in shock and hung up. In the next breath he reached blindly for Matt and hugged him hard. "You weren't wrong. She went to Salt Lake on a bus this morning."

Matt's head flew back. "You're kidding."

"I wish I were, but that gives the police something to go on."

A dozen questions filled Colt's mind.

The Wagners looked pained. "What can we do to help?" Wendie asked.

"Thanks for offering, but this is a matter for the police. I want them to find out how many other passengers on that bus were headed for Salt Lake. Maybe she has a boyfriend who talked her into going."

"No." Jen shook her head. "She would have told me."

"I thought she told me everything, too, Jen." Colt's features turned grim. "The fact that none of us, including her own twin, knew her agenda, let alone that she asked you to lie for her, tells me my daughter has some deep-seated problems. Come on, Matt. Let's go home. I'll phone the police on the way."

The Wagners walked them out to the truck. Colt gave Jen a hug before he drove off with Matt and made the call. He didn't hang up with the chief detective until they'd reached the ranch.

As he shut off the motor Matt turned to him. "Are they going to look for her?"

Colt nodded. "They'll make inquiries, but he told me not to be too worried since she bought a round-trip ticket. The Salt Lake police will be at the bus depot in the morning when she shows up, so he told me it would be a waste of my time to fly there."

"But we're going to go anyway, right?"

He'd never loved his son more than at this moment.

"Right." They walked around back and entered the house. "We'll have to leave for the airport at five. That's not very far away. I'll wake you in time."

"I don't think I'll be able to fall asleep."

"Try. We're going to need all our energy tomorrow."

Matt paused at the foot of the stairs. "Your birthday's a week after Thanksgiving. Maybe she went to Salt Lake to get you a special present."

He rubbed the knot in the back of his neck. "Don't I wish that were the reason."

Matt's expression closed up. "Why do you think she went?"

Since Mr. Padakis had first mentioned Salt Lake, Colt didn't want to admit—let alone put a voice to—an uncomfortable thought working its way through his psyche. "I don't know, Matt."

And because he didn't know, he wasn't about to speculate about something that could destroy the world he'd created for his children. He'd always believed he'd raised them in a happy emotional environment.

But if Allie's disappearance, even for a forty-eight-hour period, had anything to do with what he was thinking, then it meant he'd built his house on sand and it was too late to hold back the dreaded flood.

Matt started up the stairs. Colt watched him go. There'd be no sleep for either of them tonight.

He wandered into the living room, gravitating to a picture of his daughter on her first horse. The image blurred.

Did I fail you, Allie?

Was that what this was about?

"KATHRYN?"

"Hi, Cord. Sorry to phone you this late, but the hospital called me in on a teen runaway case. I'm going to have to cancel our ski plans for tomorrow."

"I won't pretend I'm not disappointed. I'd rather ski with you than anybody."

"I feel the same way about you. But since Kit's expecting again, she'll be thrilled to have you all to herself. Give her my love."

"I will. When you get a chance, I want to hear about your case."

"Of course, but not tonight. Get a good sleep."

Kathryn rang off, then made a call to Maggie. The moment she answered Kathryn said, "Forgive me for calling you so late. I'd like to ask a favor of you, but first I need to know your plans for tomorrow afternoon."

"Jake and I were going to stay home and play with Robbie. Kamila might come over with Jared. Why?"

"I need to take a missing teen back to her family. She's in the hospital getting over the flu and can probably go home tomorrow. But she lives in Bozeman, Montana, and—"

"You'd like me to fly you there?" she finished for Kathryn. "That's not a long flight. I'd love to do it. Meet me at the hangar at twelve-thirty. I'll have you there by two. Robbie will nap while I'm gone."

"You're the best, Maggie," Kathryn said. "I'll call you in the morning if the doctor decides she should stay in the hospital another day. Otherwise, plan on it."

"Sounds good. Do you know something?"

"What?"

"You've become a workaholic. That's how I used to be before I met Jake."

"Yeah, well, we all can't be as lucky as you."

"You could have married Steve."

"I could have, but he only proposed to me because he couldn't have you."

After a long silence, Maggie said, "What are you talking about?"

The time for honesty had come. How strange that this was the moment. "Kit's brother was already clerking for you when I arrived on the scene. It was *you* he loved. You were the reason he left California. When he asked me to marry him, I told him I was flattered, but I didn't want to be your substitute. He got all red in the face, but he didn't deny it."

"I had no idea." Her sister sounded shocked.

"Of course not. That's because you were so in love with Jake, you didn't know if you were coming or going. I can't say I blame you. Jake Halsey's the kind of man who is so attractive he gives every woman a heart attack. Unfortunately, there's only one of him. If I didn't love you so much, I'd scratch your eyes out."

Maggie laughed, then sobered. "Honestly, Kathryn, I love him so much, it scares me."

"Steve saw it, too. That's why I told him that until he went back to California to get away from you, he'd never be happy."

"So *that's* the reason he suddenly left."

"Now you know the whole truth. When I told the family I couldn't marry him because I loved him like a brother, I meant it."

She heard Maggie clear her throat. "Your turn's coming, Kathryn."

"No. I've had plenty of possible turns, but I've discovered I'm not the marrying kind. I crave my freedom too much. Maybe being a captive at Skwars Farm for twenty-six years made me claustrophobic over the whole institution. My psychiatrist says we need to explore it, but that's for another day. Talk to you tomorrow. Love you."

After she hung up, she left the empty isolation room and crossed the hall to check on Allie. The teen was asleep. Her long bus ride and the flu had left Allie on the verge of exhaustion when she'd left the depot.

Whatever had caused Allie to leave home had worn her out, physically and emotionally, but her vital signs looked good. She could be released tomorrow, but would have to stay in bed at home for another night at least till the flu had left her system.

Without wasting any more time, Kathryn slipped back across the hall to make the most important phone call of the night. It was quarter to twelve. If Allie's father suspected nothing and still thought his daughter was at her best friend's house enjoying a sleepover, then he was in for a huge shock.

But if he'd discovered she was missing and was frantically looking for her, then it was past time to end his anguish.

Allie had painted a picture of a loving family. Like Kathryn, Allie had put her father on a pedestal no other man could hold a candle to. She was an exceptional girl. It meant she had an exceptional father. There'd been no mention of a mother.

Kathryn reached for her note pad where she'd written down the phone number Allie had given her and punched in the digits.

WHILE COLT WAITED for the detective in Salt Lake to call him back, he went up to Allie's bedroom. He'd already given the police a description of what she was wearing when she'd left for school, including her backpack. Colt hoped that a thorough search of her room might reveal a clue to help him out. Anything…

She always stashed her money from odd jobs and babysitting in a drawstring purse hanging in the closet. None was there. Naturally she'd used it to buy her bus ticket. To his dismay, he found her cell phone in the bottom drawer of her dresser. She'd turned it off, killing that one glimmer of hope she might call him.

His daughter had been planning this for a long time. The pit in his stomach yawned wide.

Expecting to hear from the detective, he was ready to answer when his cell phone rang. He pulled it from his pocket and clicked on. "Detective Martinez?"

"No," sounded a female voice. "Are you Mr. Brenner?"

He blinked. "Who's this?" Colt knew he sounded terse, but couldn't help it.

"I'm Katy McFarland." Katy was the nickname she used with young people. "The first thing you need to know is that your daughter Allie is fine, but she's asleep right now. She gave me your phone number so I could call you."

Adrenaline gushed through his veins. "Where is she?" he cried out. "Who are you?"

"I'm a medical caseworker for North Avenues Hospital in Salt Lake City, Utah, and was called in when your daughter was brought here around four-thirty this afternoon. She became dizzy after getting off the Greyhound bus. A passerby saw her on the ground and called 911. There was no ID on her. An ambulance picked her up and brought her to the E.R. Your daughter has the H1N1 virus, but it's not a serious case."

Colt staggered to the bed and sank down.

"She's really all right?"

"I wouldn't lie to you, but I have to tell you her biggest fear is that you won't be able to forgive her for what she did. In case you didn't know it, she worships the ground you walk on, so that makes a girl nervous to disappoint the most wonderful father in the whole world."

She'd imitated Allie's way of speaking to perfection, charming Colt, who was close to speechless at this point. "I don't know how to thank you."

"You just did, so don't think about it anymore. We've got her on an IV to treat her flu symptoms. If she continues to improve, she can probably be released tomorrow provided she gets nursing care at home for another day."

Colt jumped to his feet. "My son was the one who figured out she'd taken the bus somewhere. The police are attempting to locate her in Salt Lake right now. Matt and I will fly to Salt Lake on the earliest flight out of Bozeman in the morning. We want to be with her until she's out of the woods."

"You don't need to do that. To be frank, your daughter didn't want to stay here tonight. She has begged me to let her go home tomorrow. In the event that she's well enough, I've made arrangements through the hospital to fly her to Bozeman by private charter in the afternoon. I'll accompany her and take care of her for another day until she's up and around."

"I can't let you do that."

"It's my job."

"No one has a job like that," he argued. "No wonder our hospitals are in financial trouble."

"The patient advocacy department is funded by a private donor, so it's not a concern. More importantly, your daughter made a deal with me. She would tell me your name and let me call you if I nursed her till she was better. We shook on it."

Good grief.

Allie, Allie. What was going on inside her? After a certain age, she'd only wanted Noreen around and Colt hadn't hired another nanny. Yet in her vulnerability today, she'd reached out to a stranger. Why?

Colt wanted to ask this woman if she knew what had driven Allie to do what she did, but now wasn't the time. It was enough to know his daughter was safe in a hospital, getting treated for the flu of all things.

He took a deep breath. "How soon can I talk to her?"

"As soon as she's awake. Housekeeping has brought me a cot so I can stay with her tonight. If she should wake up, I'll let her use my phone to call you. Otherwise, call my number in the morning and I'll put her on."

He pursed his lips. "I may phone you before that to find out if you're real or if I'm having an out-of-body experience."

She laughed quietly. A husky kind of laugh that reso-
nated inside him. "There's nothing more terrifying than
not knowing where your child is. Until you can hug her
and kiss her, I know you won't quite believe you have
her back."

Whoever this woman was, she could read minds. It
gave him goose flesh. "Ms. McFarland?"

"Yes?"

"Thank you," he whispered.

"You're welcome, Mr. Brenner. We'll talk in the
morning. Good night."

She hung up first, leaving him dazed.

When he gathered his wits, he left the room and
walked down the hall past the guest bedroom to Matt's
room. His son had fallen asleep, but after what they'd
been through, he decided to wake him up.

"Matt?" he called softly to him.

He made a sound and turned toward him. "Is it time
to go?"

Colt sat down on the side of the bed. "We don't have
to go anywhere. Your sister's been found." In the next
few minutes, he told him about the phone call.

Matt reached over and hugged him. "Do you think
I'll catch it?"

He hadn't seen that question coming. "I don't know.
Let's not worry about that now. Go back to sleep."

"They're really going to fly her home?"

"That's what the nurse said."

"Whoa. Well, good night, Dad." Matt laid back down
and punched his pillow to get it in the right position.

Colt eyed his son for a moment. The biggest care on
Matt's mind now was whether he would come down

with the virus. Would that the flu was all that plagued Colt. Unfortunately for him, this new knowledge was only the tip of an enormous iceberg.

After leaving Matt's bedroom, he headed for his study again. He called both detectives and left messages that Allie had been found. Following that, he e-mailed the Wagners to tell them the good news. There was no one else to inform.

Wired and restless, he went to the kitchen to make himself some coffee. Caffeine was the last thing he needed, but it was the only drink he wanted.

His premonition that something was wrong with Allie had borne fruit. Two times he'd experienced this. Both times there'd been bad news. He dreaded the thought of it ever happening again. His heart might not be able to take it a third time.

Noreen was going to be surprised when another woman besides herself would be waiting on Allie. Colt had gotten the surprise of *his* life when a Ms. McFarland, rather than the detective, had phoned to let him know his daughter was in hospital. Sick, but safe.

The woman had sent an essence through the phone line he couldn't describe. He had to confess that his curiosity had been aroused. For several reasons, he knew it would be a long time before tomorrow afternoon rolled around.

Colt wasn't sure he could wait. If he talked to Allie in the morning and didn't hear improvement, then he'd fly to Salt Lake with Matt as planned.

KATHRYN HAD SET her watch alarm for six-thirty. After she got up from the cot, she checked her patient's vital signs. Everything looked good. Her temperature was down to ninety-nine. While Allie still slept, she stepped outside to use the restroom and freshen up. She ordered breakfast trays for both of them, then put on a new surgical mask.

As she reached the room, the E.R. doctor was just coming out. "She's doing fine. Keep her on the IV until you're ready to transport her."

"I've arranged it for this afternoon."

He nodded his approval before walking away.

Kathryn went back in the room. "Good morning."

Allie looked happy to see her. "Hi."

"The doctor said you're coming right along. Let's get you up to the bathroom, then you'll feel even better."

"I've never had to go so badly."

"That's what an IV does to you." She raised the head of her bed, then helped her get up and walk to the bathroom while she rolled the IV stand. "Do you feel dizzy?"

"Not really."

"Good, but I'm still going to stay right outside the door. If you start to feel funny, just tell me."

"Okay."

When Allie came out again, she said, "I feel ten pounds lighter."

Kathryn laughed. "You probably are. Need help getting back to bed?"

"I don't think so."

To her relief, Allie made it without support. "Do you feel any nausea this morning?"

"No. I'm hungry."

"I'm glad to hear that." She helped ease her back

on the bed. "Our breakfast should be here in a minute. While we wait, why don't you call your father. I promised him you would."

"I'm afraid to."

Kathryn made a face. "Afraid? Of the most wonderful father in the whole world?"

"By now I'm sure he knows I asked Jen to lie for me. I think Dad hates lies more than anything else."

"But he loves *you* more than anything else, Allie. Once you tell him the reason behind this incident and let him know you're sorry for not being honest with him, he'll understand and love you all the more." She pulled out the phone and pressed his number. "Here. It's ringing."

With reluctance Allie took the phone from her. Almost immediately she said, "Hi, Dad. It's me." Whatever he answered in response caused the tears to roll down her cheeks. "I miss you, too. I'm so sorry for what I did."

Kathryn slipped out in the hall to give them privacy. The trays eventually arrived. She took them in the room and put them on the table that slid over the bed. Propping herself on the stool, Kathryn reached for hers and devoured her toast and eggs. In a few minutes, she heard Allie saying goodbye.

"I love you, too. Here she is." She extended the phone to Kathryn. "Dad wants to talk to you."

She took it from her and put her empty tray on the side table. "Good morning, Mr. Brenner."

"It is now." His voice sounded deeper.

"Are you grounded yet?" she teased.

He chuckled. "Almost. Like you said, it will take hugging her to convince me completely."

"The doctor says she can go home. If all goes well, we should be in Bozeman by two."

"That's even earlier than I'd hoped."

The man couldn't wait to get his daughter back. "She can't get home fast enough either. We'll be coming in on a Cessna CJ2."

"All the comforts of home for my daughter. I'm very grateful."

"I'm thrilled she's doing this well. Before we hang up, there is one thing. Allie stowed her backpack in one of the lockers at the bus depot, but the receipt with the access code for the computer was stolen along with her purse. I'm afraid you're the only person who can authorize someone to open it."

"I'll take care of it right now and ask them to ship it back to us."

"Hopefully by the time she's ready to return to school, it will have arrived. See you in about six hours."

"I'm counting down the time."

The comment made her smile. She hung up.

"Katy?"

Bemused by his comment, she was slow to flick her gaze to Allie. "What is it?"

"I'm glad you're going to be taking care of me."

"You are?"

She nodded. "People die from the H1N1 virus."

The poor thing had been so frightened to tell her father what she'd done, she was only now realizing the state of her health.

"Well, it's not going to happen on my watch. While

you graze the TV channels, I'm going to go home and pack a few things. Then I'll be back. I expect your breakfast to be gone."

"I want to eat."

"Good. You know the button to press if you need a nurse to help you to the bathroom again. Can I get you anything else before I go?"

"No. Just hurry."

"I promise."

Nancy had gone off shift when Kathryn approached the desk. Sue was on duty. Kathryn caught her up to speed on the Brenner case, then she left the hospital for home.

It was cold and cloudy, but no storm was pending yet. For Allie's sake she hoped there'd be little turbulence on the flight to Montana.

Once she'd reached her condo, she packed a suitcase, then took a shower and washed her hair. After she'd blow-dried it, she slipped on fresh underwear and walked over to the closet.

She gave a few outfits consideration, then made her choice of a pair of camel-colored wool pants and matching cashmere sweater with a crew neck. She toned it with a dark brown suede blazer she'd picked up with her family in Rio. The suede boots in the same tone were comfortable, yet dressy. Her topaz studs added the right touch.

The clothes she'd worn at the farm had been nothing like the outfits Maggie wore. Her sister, with her long legs and slim figure, looked like a fashion model without even trying. With her sense of dress, she'd helped put a wardrobe together that suited Kathryn. Their family's local and national prominence dictated that they be ready for the camera whenever they went out in public.

Both sisters were blonde and five foot eight, but Kathryn's figure was a little fuller. Sometimes from farther off, people thought the two of them were twins. But once they got up close, the differences in their facial features became evident.

Kathryn had a wider smile and naturally dark-fringed eyes. Since becoming a mother, Maggie wore her hair shorter, the way Kathryn had done at the farm. Now they'd reversed things.

She rummaged through her accessories drawer and pulled out a chiffon scarf in a geometric design of leopard-skin colors. Once she'd caught her shoulder-length blond hair at the nape with it, she applied a pink frost lipstick, sprayed herself with her favorite wildflower scent and was ready.

Before she left the condo, she phoned her parents. Her mother answered. "I'm so glad you called, darling. Come on over and have lunch with us."

"I wish I could, but I'm on a case and won't be home for a few days." Her mom understood what that meant. Any lost child took top priority. Thanks to her psychiatrist's suggestion, Kathryn found that if she took the time to explain things to her mother, she didn't get so upset if Kathryn couldn't be with them.

"Where are you going?"

"I'm taking a teenager home to her family in Bozeman. Her name is Allie Brenner. She came down with the H1N1 virus, but it's a light case. Maggie's going to fly us there in a little while."

"Was she a kidnap victim?"

"No. She came to Salt Lake for a reason, but didn't tell her father where she was going. He thought she was at school."

"Oh, dear."

"When she got off the Greyhound bus she became dizzy. Someone called the police and she was taken to the hospital without any ID or money. She wouldn't tell anyone anything. That's why I was called in."

"The poor child."

"My feeling exactly. Something's going on with her, Mom. I have no idea why she came here, but she finally trusted me enough to let me contact her father."

"He must have been out of his mind with grief."

Kathryn would never forget the way he'd answered the phone. Talk about a terrified parent. "He was…and so grateful for the call."

"Of course. No one knows better than I what that phone call was like when Maggie told us she'd found *you!*" Her mother broke down weeping.

Afraid it would get her started, Kathryn said, "Allie's frightened, too, and for some reason is clinging to me. Since she needs watching, I decided to see her back safely."

"Well—" her mother sniffed "—you and Maggie take care. Call us when you get there."

"I promise. Love you, Mom."

Chapter Three

The gleaming white-and-blue Cessna with gold strip-
ing stood out from the overcast sky as it descended and
made seamless contact with the runway. Colt had been
given permission to drive his Xterra as close as the rules
allowed to pick up his daughter.

Matt whistled. "Sweet. How would it be to own one
of those?"

Colt agreed, but right now he'd focused his gaze on
the door, waiting for it to open. The second there was
movement, he started forward.

"Allie!" he cried when he saw her in the aperture
wearing her parka.

"Hi, Dad!"

He took the last steps to reach her and pulled her into
his arms. She gave him a squeeze that almost knocked
his hat off. "Do you have any idea how happy I am to
see you?" Without letting her go, he carried her the
small distance to the car. Matt opened the rear door so
Colt could help her into the seat. He kissed her forehead.
"Are you all right?"

"Yes, but I'm glad to be home."

"Amen to that." In a second he had her strapped in. "I'll be right back."

When he started for the plane again, his breath caught at the sight of the stunning blonde woman who'd just stepped out on the tarmac. Impressions of caramel swirls among vanilla cream flew at him like reflections off a glacier sparkling in the sun.

She was the epitome of feminine elegance, the kind of trait a few women were born with that had nothing to do with what they wore. Although what she was wearing was perfect down to the shape of her slim waist shown off in a suede jacket. It drew his attention to her womanly hips and long legs. A white parka lay over one arm. She held a small suitcase in her other hand.

"Whoa," his son murmured behind him. Matt was old enough to appreciate the sight of a truly gorgeous woman.

His comment said it all, jerking Colt back to his senses. He reached for her suitcase. "Welcome to Montana, Ms. McFarland. I'm Colton Brenner. This is Allie's brother, Matt."

Her startling blue eyes shifted to his son. "How are you, Matt?" She shook his hand. "Did anyone ever tell you that you and Allie look a lot alike? Except you're the handsome one."

While Colt chuckled, a warm blush spread over Matt's face. "Call me Katy."

For some reason she didn't look like a Katy to him. "Matt? If you'll help her in the front seat, I'll stow this in the back. Let me have your parka."

"Thank you." As she handed it to him, their arms brushed. He could smell her fragrance. All of it was unexpected, increasing an unbidden awareness of her. Colt didn't like it. He'd never experienced such a strong reaction to a woman before, not even when— A grimace marred his features. *Just don't think, Brenner.*

Out of the corner of his eye he saw her climb in the backseat next to Allie. She had a mind of her own. It was just as well. Now she wouldn't be seated next to him to provide a distraction he didn't need while he took them home.

He walked around and got in behind the wheel. As he drove away, he could see the Cessna taxiing out in preparation for takeoff. "You people have provided an amazing service for our family. You'll have to tell me where I can send a contribution."

"That's very generous of you, but the patient advocacy program is in place for that very purpose. The only thing of importance is that your daughter is back with you safe and sound."

And troubled.

He glanced over his shoulder at Allie. "I was worried about your cold, honey. We should have done something about it a few days ago."

"A lot of my friends have had one. Do you think they've had the H1N1, Katy?"

"Probably. We might not have known about you if you hadn't taken that long bus trip. It exhausted you and caused your temperature to spike."

Colt turned onto the highway headed toward the ranch. "Next time you're sick, I'm not waiting to get you in to see the doctor."

"I'm sorry about everything. Hey, Katy? Do you think Matt will catch it?"

Colt's eyes met their guest's amused gaze through the rearview mirror. It was only a moment, but he felt a connection. The same kind of feeling he'd experienced with her over the phone. He gripped the steering wheel tighter.

"Tell you what. If he gets a cold, your father can take him in to be tested."

"I'm not going to get it," Matt grumbled.

Time for a change of subject. "Noreen is fixing your favorite dinner. I hope you'll be able to eat a little of it."

"Breakfast tasted good, and I ate part of my lunch."

"Sounds like your appetite has picked up. I don't think you ate a solid meal all week."

"That's because my throat was sore. Do you like enchiladas, Katy?"

"I adore them. In fact, I could live on Mexican food."

Matt leaned forward. "That's what *you* always say, Dad."

Colt stepped on the gas. The sooner they reached the ranch where they weren't all trapped together, the better.

"Is it hard learning how to be a nurse?" Allie asked.

"Only if you have trouble with math and chemistry."

"I guess *you* didn't," Matt said.

"But I'm a klutz at logic. My last boyfriend showed me his LSAT books. I took some of the sample quizzes and failed them."

"What does LSAT mean?"

"It's a test to see if you can get in to law school."

"I didn't know that. Give us an example."

"It's hard to think of one."

"Try." To Colt's astonishment, Matt was being amazingly persistent.

"Okay. Let's say a person in a cold climate buys a stylish coat, even though it doesn't keep him warm. You assume this person will sacrifice comfort for appearance, right?"

They both said yes.

"So then you have to read five different situations to see which one the same assumption applies to. But it's hard and tricky. For example, an acrobat asks the circus to buy him an expensive outfit to impress the audience. Do you think that's the same thing?"

Silence reigned. Finally Allie said, "I don't get it."

"Neither do I. Did you, Dad?"

"Well, let's think about it. The guy in the cold climate needed some kind of a coat, warm or not. The acrobat didn't need an expensive outfit. Any kind of outfit would have worked."

"I still don't get it."

"Neither do I," Katy assured him. "My brain doesn't work like your father's or Steve's. As I said earlier, trying to do his homework was worse than figuring out a Chinese puzzle."

Both his children laughed and kept on chatting with her.

Steve. Her latest boyfriend out of how many? What was she? Mid-twenties? Her age was hard to tell.

She was a catalyst, stirring up conversations they'd

never had, prompting them to ask questions they wouldn't have thought of. *Disturbing the peace and tranquility of his well-ordered life.*

KATHRYN NOTICED her host let his children carry the conversation the rest of the way to the ranch. They traveled under a low ceiling of clouds. She was glad they'd beaten the latest storm front.

At the entrance to the Circle B, he turned off the main road and they began the climb through a mountain fairyland flocked with snow. It spoke to her heart of hearts.

She felt it happening again. That spurt of adrenaline racing through her body.

The first time she'd experienced it was at the plane when she'd seen the tall rancher striding toward her wearing well-worn cowboy boots and a black Stetson. Rugged, powerful. She'd immediately thought, *here* was a man to match his mountains.

Over the years at Skwars Farm, she'd roomed with many families in a rotation. The last family she'd been with had a daughter, Nelly, close to Kathryn's age. Nelly had a driver's license and could take the family car into town. She always stopped at the library to bring back more Louis L'Amour books for Kathryn, who'd gotten hooked on *High Lonesome* years earlier.

Ever since Kathryn had been old enough to fantasize, she'd pretended to be Considine's woman. Considine was the hard-hitting outlaw whose code of honor in the face of all odds helped him survive on the American frontier.

Talk about an out-of-body experience—just a little

while ago he'd come to life in the form of Colton Brenner.

Fantasizing was a tool Kathryn had used to survive during her twenty-six years in captivity. Her psychiatrist couldn't emphasize often enough that it played the key role in helping her cope during the years she was floundering.

But it had been four years since her family had found her and she still couldn't shut off the mechanism that caused her to dream beyond the boundaries of reality. Staring at Colton Brenner, imagining he was the hero of her young girl's dreams, wasn't healthy.

Already she sensed this twenty-first-century family man had staked out his own territory a long time ago. Only a special few had entrée into his inner circle. Kathryn got the distinct impression she was an unwanted guest here, existing on borrowed time because of an unexpected turn of events involving Allie. If nothing else, his set boundaries guaranteed an end to her flights of fantasy, breaking the dangerous quarter-of-a-century cycle.

The car wound around one more curve in the road lined with walls of dense evergreens covered in snow. Suddenly they came upon a vale nestled between the mountains containing a fabulous western-style ranch house. Smoke curled from the chimney.

She picked out the barn, the bunkhouses and bungalows, another house, outbuildings, pens and corrals. In the far distance, she saw the stream that crossed the property and beyond it a herd of cattle.

"We're home, Katy."

"I can see that." She squeezed the teen's arm. "I've

decided the name Circle B doesn't do this place justice. It should be called something evocative like Cloud Bottom Ranch."

Everyone in the car laughed, even the children's father. He said, "Our ancestors started what was then called the Ayrshire Ranch on just six hundred acres and a little bungalow. They hoped to raise Ayrshire dairy cows, but the experiment didn't last long.

"Each generation of Brenners that followed bought other small parcels of land and grew crops. It got renamed the Circle B after my great-grandfather brought in Angus cattle. No one could pronounce Ayrshire properly anyway. He wanted something simple and straightforward."

She smiled, remembering the problems people had with names like her kidnapper Antonin Buric and the Skwars families. "Americans do have a way of slaughtering most languages." Once again, the twins roared with laughter.

Through the rearview mirror, she felt their father's gaze. "As the ranch began to prosper, the Circle B stuck, but I must admit your fanciful version captures its true essence. Interestingly enough, the Sioux and Shoshone had two names for this area depending on the season. In winter they called it 'Walkway to the Clouds.'"

Kathryn felt a little shiver race across her skin. "How beautiful." He nodded. "And summer?"

"Valley of the Flowers."

Another Albion Basin. Just like home.

More stuff fantasies were made of, but she was through with those. Realizing the car had stopped, she undid her seat belt and leaned across to help Allie. "I bet bed sounds good about now."

"It does."

"I thought so."

Matt opened the door for Kathryn while their father picked up his daughter and carried her around the end of the house. Kathryn alighted from the car with her purse. "Thanks, Matt."

"Sure." He opened the trunk to get her parka and suitcase. "Follow me."

The two-story ranch house had been constructed of dark wood and local stone. At the back, there was a large covered veranda with picture windows facing an eastern exposure.

Matt showed her through the door into a room to wash hands and stow boots and parkas. He hung hers on a peg, then walked her down a hall that opened into a vaulted great room dominated by the rock fireplace. On either side were huge, tall picture windows looking out on the mountains. This had to be the heart of their home.

"I'll take your suitcase upstairs and be right back, Katy."

"Thanks, Matt."

The comfortable brown leather couches and chairs with colorful woven throws invited her to curl up. Framed family pictures covered one wall. Her eyes wandered over the floor-to-ceiling bookcase filled with books, games and an entertainment center. Dark honey-colored hardwood floors not covered by oriental rugs gleamed in the firelight.

She gravitated to the fire's warmth, eager to look at every photo and examine the titles.

"Welcome to the Circle B, Ms. McFarland. I'm Noreen Walters."

Kathryn swung around. The older brunette woman was probably in her fifties. Hearty-looking. Attractive. "How do you do." She shook hands with her. "From what I hear, nobody could get along without you and your husband."

"That's nice to know. How's my girl?"

"She's going to be fine, but needs bed rest and liquids with her medication. I'm really superfluous, except for checking her vitals. The one thing we don't want is to find she's getting respiratory problems or see her temperature elevate. It's been hovering between ninety-nine and a hundred since last night. I'm anticipating it will get back to normal by tomorrow."

"That little monkey fought her father about her cold."

"Isn't that why they call it the terrible teens?"

Noreen chuckled. "Do you have children?"

"No. I'm not married. What about you?"

A shadow marred her expression. "I had three miscarriages before we came to work for Colton."

Kathryn felt her pain. "Now you have two remarkable children."

The shadow disappeared. "Yes."

"I fear there are times when she thinks she has a stubborn third one." Her host's deep voice prompted Kathryn to turn around.

"You mean four," Noreen quipped. "You forgot Ed."

He smiled, then said, "I think we'll plan to eat dinner

around six. That should give Allie time for a good nap."

Noreen nodded. "If you're hungry now, Ms. McFarland, I'll send Matt up with a tray for you."

"Thank you, but I ate before we flew here. And please...call me Katy."

"I will," she said before leaving the room.

"While we're on the subject of names, mine is Colt."

It suited him down to the last irreverent tendril curling against his neck.

Kathryn had discovered that without the Stetson, he had a head of shocking black hair whose ends wanted to wave. The arrangement of hard-boned features made him a striking man. Brows of the same black shade framed his eyes. They were the color of spring grass and looked translucent in the fire's glow.

His eyes took swift inventory of her. She could hardly breathe.

Without conscious thought her gaze drifted over the rest of him. He wore a long-sleeved, plaid flannel shirt in blues and greens. The hem was tucked into jeans that molded powerful thighs. His hard-muscled physique revealed a man who kept fit in the outdoors.

There was an aura about him, a mental toughness and discipline she'd sensed beneath the male veneer. You didn't trifle with a man like him.

Allie knew it. She'd been raised by him.

Kathryn no longer questioned why his daughter had been afraid to call him from the hospital. Yet her reason for disappointing him had to have been so compelling that she'd been willing to risk it.

Though the subject hadn't been brought up by the twins or their father, Kathryn suspected this situation had everything to do with their mother. No one had talked about her or mentioned her, but it was clear Colt Brenner's woman—whether she'd been his wife or not, whether she was alive or not—was the elephant in the room.

"I need to take Allie's vitals. I'll just get the things I need out of my suitcase."

"The twins' bedrooms are on the next floor," Colt said. "The upstairs guest bedroom is between them. I'll show you."

She followed him to the foyer and up the staircase to the next floor. He moved with natural male grace. Aware her thoughts were too concentrated on him, she looked around her. The interior was an amalgamation of refined rustic and contemporary design. "You've created the perfect mountain home."

"Thank you. We used to live in the original house on the property. Now Noreen and Ed live there."

He opened the door to her room, which was decorated in earth tones with hardwood floors. She found her suitcase at the end of the queen-size bed covered with a patchwork quilt. After retrieving the bag inside it, she accompanied him to the bedroom on the left.

Matt was spread across the end of Allie's queen talking to his sister. It reminded her of the way Kathryn's brothers sometimes did that with her.

"Hi!" they said in unison. Matt stood up.

The sunny room with accents of blue and white delighted her. She moved to the side of the bed and sat down. "Shall we get this over with? Then you can rest."

Kathryn listened to her lungs with her stethoscope. They sounded clear. Her blood pressure was normal. Her pulse was a little fast; that didn't surprise her. Allie had expended extra energy for the flight.

She slipped the digital thermometer under her arm. After it beeped she read, "Ninety-nine!" Kathryn flashed her a smile. "You're going to live." She could tell her pronouncement relieved Colt.

Someone had put a pitcher of water and a glass on the side table. She got up and poured a full glass before handing her the pills she needed to take. "Drink all of it."

"Okay."

After she swallowed them, Kathryn asked, "Have you been to the bathroom?"

"Dad helped me." Her brown eyes darted to her father. "Could I call Jen first?"

He shook his dark head. "She phoned earlier today and I told her you'd get in touch with her tomorrow." In a surprise move, he reached into her bottom dresser drawer and pulled out a cell phone. "I'll turn this on in case you need to phone me." Colt put it on her side table.

If Kathryn wasn't mistaken, Allie looked guilty about her phone. She'd obviously hidden it before leaving for Salt Lake. At least the thief hadn't gotten hold of it when he'd taken her purse. "Is she mad at me?"

"I think it's more of a case of her being mad at herself for going along with you."

Allie averted her eyes. "I'll apologize to her."

"I think that better include her parents."

"I bet they hate me." Kathryn detected a tremor in her voice.

"Not their daughter's best friend," Colt assured her with a kiss on the cheek. "Sleep tight, honey."

Kathryn gathered up her bag and the three of them left the room. Colt turned to her. "There's an en suite bathroom in your room. After you've freshened up, feel free to come downstairs and watch TV or do whatever you'd like. I have work to do, but I'll ask Noreen to make you coffee or tea, whichever you prefer."

"If you have a cola, I'd like that."

"I'll get it for you," Matt offered.

"Thanks. I'll be down in a minute."

The second she found herself alone and closed the door, her breath came rushing out. Until just now she hadn't realized she'd been holding it. There was no one to blame but Colt Brenner for her body's uncharacteristic reaction.

Afraid to dwell on thoughts of him, she put her bag down and reached for the phone to call her mother because she'd promised. When her mom didn't answer, she left a message on her voice mail that she'd arrived safely.

After she hung up, she saw that she'd received several work messages and one from Maggie. Her pulse raced, fearing something might be wrong. Kathryn phoned her immediately, anxious to hear her sister's voice.

"Kathryn?"

"Maggie? What's happened?"

"Why nothing. I'm driving through Federal Heights right now, but couldn't wait to talk to you."

Kathryn frowned. "About what?"

"You know what. I was the one who opened the plane door. I stood right behind you when Mr. Tall, Dark and Handsome reached for his daughter. My jaw must have dropped a foot. It's a good thing Jake didn't see my reaction."

Heat crept into Kathryn's cheeks.

"Cat got your tongue? I thought so. When you find it, call me back."

Click.

Oh, Maggie. If only it were that simple…

He was spectacular all right, but there was layer after complicated layer to Colt Brenner, the man.

On the surface she understood the protective father and successful rancher, yet already Kathryn had picked up on negative vibes he sent out.

Her radar had been fine-tuned in Wisconsin. She was good at reading what was going on in other people's heads. She'd had to be after having been passed around to different homes month after month, year after year.

No one had wanted the little girl who'd been dumped on them at the farm, but they did their duty. She'd been tolerated and taken care of, but she'd been the proverbial rolling stone, gathering no moss.

The same thing was happening to her now, only this time it was Colt Brenner doing his duty. For his daughter's sake, he was tolerating Kathryn, taking care of her needs, but he didn't like being dumped on. Allie's behavior had placed him in an impossible position.

Allie had put Kathryn in an impossible position, too!

What Colt didn't realize was that Kathryn didn't

like it, either, but she didn't take his hostility personally. Through years of dealing with similar situations on the farm, she'd learned not to do that because she understood those families had no vested interest in her. She was a temporary encumbrance until the end of the month when she was happily shifted to someone else's household.

Her only comfort had come from playing with the youngest children, who were more accepting of her presence in their lives. Unlike the adults, they didn't see her as an intrusion. She knew Matt Brenner didn't see her that way.

During the rest of her stay here, she'd befriend him. If he was still downstairs, she'd ask him to help her do one of those puzzles she'd seen on the shelf. Besides hard work and her fantasizing, books and puzzles had helped save her life growing up.

It had grown dark on the way back from the lower pasture. Colt had driven there to haul more feed, but as it turned out, the trip hadn't been necessary. His stockmen had taken care of it.

He'd used the excuse of work to bolt from the house. Sixteen years ago, he'd been a naive twenty-year-old who'd gotten sidetracked by a woman's magic and didn't suspect the ugliness of what it masked until it was too late.

Never again.

The lights from the ranch house beckoned him. While he'd been gone, the wind had picked up. It brought snow flurries portending the storm that had moved in over the mountains. On nights like this, he always experienced a warm feeling of homecoming, but tonight he was aware of an added element because *she* was inside.

Colt ground his teeth. He wanted Ms. McFarland out of his house and off his land.

The scene that greeted him as he walked in the great room a few minutes later was so domestic and cozy, it caused an upheaval inside him.

"Hey, Dad? Come and look! Now that you're back you can help us put my puzzle of Brett Favre together." Favre was Matt's hero. Allie had bought him the thousand-piece version of the pro quarterback wearing his Vikings jersey and helmet after his football banquet. Colt had planned to work on it with the kids this weekend.

Their guest's hair gleamed like spun gold in the fire-light. She seemed to be concentrating hard. In fact, she didn't look up as he walked over to the card table Matt had set up in front of the fireplace. For some reason, it set off a rare burst of anger he needed to squelch. "First I need to check on Allie."

"Katy did it a little while ago. She was still asleep."

A pair of blue eyes flicked his way. They looked as hot as the fire, yet Kathryn's response was degrees cooler. "You don't need to be concerned. So far she's holding her own."

He took a fortifying breath. "That's good to hear. I'll let Noreen know I'm back so she can put dinner on."

"Allie shouldn't come downstairs before tomorrow. To save Noreen the trouble, maybe you and Matt could take a plate up to her room and eat with her?"

"What are you going to do?" Matt voiced the question on Colt's mind.

"I'll go up and get her ready, then I have some

business to do over the phone. Later on, I'll come down to the kitchen. But if it will put Noreen out…"

"Why would it?" Colt blurted before he realized he was sounding terse again. "While you're here, treat this house as your own."

"Thank you." She got up from the chair. "I'll help you finish this later, Matt."

"Great!"

Colt tried not to watch her leave the room, but the way she moved on those long legs mesmerized him. It didn't matter what she wore or the way she did her hair. She was a knockout, but he knew so much more lay beneath the surface of Ms. McFarland once you got past her initial beauty.

"She knows almost as much about football as a guy. She says her dad lives for the NFL games." Was that a fact. "She likes college football better, though. The Utes are her favorite team."

"Well, they would be, wouldn't they? Coming from Utah?" He headed for the kitchen. Matt followed.

"Yeah, except she says a lot of people like the BYU. They hate each other, especially because the Utes made the BCS twice. Her dad took her to the game they won against Alabama. Isn't that cool? She said her favorite player was Paul Kruger. He went to the NFL and plays for the Jets."

Colt couldn't remember the last time he'd heard his son this chatty. They found Noreen. "We're going to eat upstairs with Allie." He pulled three plates from the cupboard.

"What about Katy?"

"She'll come down for something later," Matt

explained before Colt could get a word in edgewise. "She's got work to do."

"What kind of work?"

"I don't know. She helps people."

Noreen was waiting for a more substantial answer. Colt started serving up the enchiladas. "Ms. McFarland works for the patient advocacy program at the hospital in Salt Lake."

"Imagine them flying her here with Allie. It's a huge expense."

Matt got some sodas out of the fridge. "She says she's a specialty nurse, kind of like some people have their own sports trainer."

Colt had trouble believing any of this had happened. "Have we got everything?"

"Yup. Let's go. I'm starving!"

"Thanks, Noreen," Colt murmured. "This looks delicious. Isn't Ed eating?"

"He'll be here in a minute. Let's hope Allie's hungry."

Colt put everything on a tray. Matt brought the drinks and they left the kitchen. At the top of the stairs he saw light beneath the closed door of the guest bedroom. He had to give Katy full marks for doing her job and being unobtrusive.

When he walked in Allie's room, she was sitting up in bed with the light on waiting for them. "Hi, honey. How are you feeling?"

"Good."

"Ready for dinner?"

Allie nodded as the two of them proceeded to wait on her. Finally they pulled up chairs and everyone started to eat. Colt was glad to see Allie finish off one of her enchiladas and dig into her salad. She was definitely getting better.

"Dad? While Katy's not in here, I want to ask you something."

"Go ahead."

"Thanksgiving's only four days away. Would it be all right if I asked her to stay with us until the weekend?"

He stopped chewing. His daughter didn't really just ask him that.

"Yeah, Dad," Matt chimed in. "In case I get sick she'll be here to take care of me. Besides, it'll take that long for us to finish the puzzle."

Putting down his fork before he made mincemeat of the rest of his enchilada, he said, "I'm afraid not, honey. Have you forgotten your uncle Bob and aunt Sherry have invited us to go to Butte for Thanksgiving? Your cousins are looking forward to it."

"They won't care if Katy comes. Aunt Sherry would really like her and she always has company stay over."

"Not this time. We have to think of Ms. McFarland, who's on loan from the hospital. No doubt she's in her room right now making plans for her next case. We can't expect to take advantage of her services like that, not after what she's done to help you."

His daughter's face fell. "I don't think I can eat any more."

Colt groaned. His daughter could manipulate when she wanted to, but this was going too far. He refused to fall for it. "That's all right. Tomorrow you'll probably be able to move around and work up more of an appetite."

In the silence that followed, he noticed his son had stopped chirping away. He'd chosen sides and had moved to Allie's corner. Colt continued to finish his meal. *Nip it in the bud.* That motto had served him well in the past.

His gaze flicked to Matt's plate. "Aren't you going to eat your apple pie?"

"Maybe later."

"Then I'll eat it now so we don't disappoint Noreen." So saying, he finished it off. While his children eyed him soulfully, he got up and put all the plates on the tray. "I'll be back in a few minutes."

Chapter Four

"Thanks for manning the desk for me, Donna. If my patient is better tomorrow, I'll fly to Salt Lake tomorrow evening and be at work Monday morning to give you a break. I know you want to get ready for Thanksgiving."

"That would great. If I can get all the shopping done Monday, then I'll cook a little at a time until the big day."

"How many are you having for dinner?"

"Twenty. Todd's brother and his wife and children are coming. What about you?"

"We're all getting together at Mom and Dad's." Thanksgiving at the McFarlands' was sacrosanct, not only for her family but for Kathryn. Until she'd been found, Thanksgiving and Christmas had been the most dreaded times of life to get through.

"I bet your family still can't believe you're home with them."

"Sometimes I can't, either."

"Not to change the subject, but you did ask. Another AMBER Alert has gone out. This time on a seven-year-old girl in Sandy named Whitney."

Kathryn's eyes closed tightly. She felt as if she'd been kicked in the stomach. "When?"

"About two hours ago. She got separated from her mother at a toy store in the South Towne Mall. It was packed with preseason shoppers. The woman's in agony."

Whitney would be in worse condition if she wasn't dead already. "Did you contact my mom?"

"Yes. She's already on it."

That was probably why her mother hadn't picked up earlier. "I wish I were there to help." But Allie had needed help, too. She still did, but not the kind Kathryn could provide.

The teen had serious issues only her father could work on with her once she found the courage to talk to him.

"You're just like your sister before she met Jake. She always wished she could be in ten places at once."

"She's still like that inside, but being a wife and mother has changed her life." Donna had started working for Maggie at the Foundation ten years ago and continued to be a good family friend, as well as an invaluable assistant, to Kathryn. "Keep me posted, will you?"

"When I hear anything new, I'll call you. Bye for now."

Kathryn hung up. If the little girl wasn't found, it could mean days, months, even years of unrelieved suffering. But she needed to set that care aside while she dealt with Allie.

When Kathryn entered the bedroom, the teen was

curled up on her side toward the window. Her shoulders were shaking beneath the covers. "Allie?"

She turned over. Kathryn could tell she was crying and rushed over to her. "Are you feeling worse?"

"No."

"Then what's wrong?"

"Everything."

Kathryn sank down on the side of the bed next to her, smoothing Allie's hair off her forehead. "Did you eat dinner?"

"Half of it." Half was better than nothing. "Katy? What are you doing for Thanksgiving?"

Where had that question come from? "I'm going to be with my family. What about you?"

"We're going to our aunt and uncle's in Butte to be with our cousins."

"That sounds fun."

Allie sat up in bed, wiping her eyes. "So you don't have to work?" Another question that had completely ignored Kathryn's comment.

"No."

"Then you could go with us, right? Dad said you'd be working with another patient so we couldn't ask you."

Her father had told Allie what any parent would have said in response, but in Colt Brenner's case there was much more to it than that. "What he meant was, I'd be busy with my work even if I stopped to have dinner with my family, and he'd be right."

"You mean you have to be at the hospital on Thanksgiving?"

"No. I do all kinds of jobs."

"Like what?"

"It's a long story. Where do you keep your brush? While I do your hair, I'll tell you."

"It's in the bathroom in the top left drawer."

"I'll be right back."

Kathryn slid off the bed and went to fetch it. After she came back, she said, "Turn your back toward me."

"Okay."

She gathered the glossy skein of hair in her hands and got started.

"That feels good."

"It's supposed to. Now to answer your question. I help my brother at the halfway house I told you about. Some of the homeless women have children. I do periodic health checks on all of them and work with him and his staff to help the adults find work and housing. Do you remember that brochure I gave you?"

She nodded.

"It talked about the McFarland Foundation. In the plaza where my condo is, there's a whole area on the ground floor where the foundation headquarters are located. My sister used to be in charge of it. Now I am, but of course I have people to help me.

"As soon as we receive word that a child has gone missing, we assist the police by sending out our own rescue people. We do ground and air searches and have resources to help find people who are lost to their families.

"When the hospital phoned me about you, it was because the police had brought you into the E.R. as a Jane Doe. That meant you couldn't be identified yet and could be a possible runaway or kidnap victim who'd either gotten away or had been let go. Every E.R. in every hospital in Salt Lake Valley knows to call the foundation if a Jane or John Doe is brought in."

Allie's turned her head. "Does it happen a lot?"

"More than you know."

"That's awful."

"I agree. After I was reunited with my family, I watched my sister doing all the things I do now. When I lived at Skwars Farm, I used to dream about becoming a doctor, but knew it was only a dream. But after I was found and was able to go to college, I changed my mind about being a doctor."

"How come?"

"Because then I wouldn't be able to be as free to do everything for the foundation that has to be done. So I became a nurse, but I'm on my own, so to speak."

"Is your sister a nurse, too?"

"No. She's an attorney who helps people who are trying to avoid bankruptcy." She was also a crack pilot.

"Does it make you feel bad you couldn't do the LSAT like she did?"

Kathryn broke into laughter. "Heavens, no. For one thing, I never wanted to be a lawyer. For another, I love what I do. As for my sister, she's superwoman and I adore her."

"I wish I had a sister."

"You've got Matt. That's even better. Think of all the cute guys he brings around."

A little laugh came out of her. "I'm glad you're my nurse."

"So am I."

"Your father must make a lot of money to pay for everything."

"Our family can thank my great-grandfather John McFarland four greats back for that. He was Utah's Copper King. He amassed a fortune worth hundreds of millions of dollars that he invested."

"I can't imagine that much money."

"Neither can I, Allie. He had mansions in London, France, New York and Salt Lake. My father makes sure it gets spent helping other people."

"Like that program you work for?"

"Exactly."

"No wonder you love him so much."

"He and my mother work together. They're awesome," she said, using the teenage vernacular.

"So's my dad." Suddenly Allie moved so her back rested against the headboard. She drew up her pajama-clad knees and locked her arms around them. "My mom left after Matt and I were born."

Ah...

Kathryn put the brush on the table and sank down on the side of the bed again. "How often do you see her?"

Allie stared at her out of pained brown eyes. "We've never met her."

An unseen hand squeezed Kathryn's heart. *Never?*

"Dad met her in Las Vegas when he was a big rodeo champion on the circuit, but they broke up after Matt and I were born. Dad thought she might have gone back to her aunt and uncle's in Salt Lake where she was raised, but he never saw or heard from her again."

"Allie…" Kathryn reached out and rocked her in her arms.

"At least when your family found you, you knew your mother loved you," Allie sobbed.

At least I knew that…

"All my friends have moms except me. Dad can't talk about it and Matt won't talk about it."

"So you decided to find your mother's aunt and uncle and talk to them." It made too much sense.

"Yes. Dad said they managed the Beehive Motel near the airport. I was going to take a taxi there, but then I got sick and that guy stole my purse with my money. I was hoping you'd stay through Thanksgiving and help me. Maybe phone them and talk to them for me since you do things like that all the time. Even if they don't know where she is, maybe they'll tell you something that would help and we could find my mom together. I just need to ask her why she didn't want me and Matt."

Good heavens. Kathryn slowly let go of her. From here on out, she had to be careful what she said to this fragile girl.

"The thing is," Allie added, "I don't want Dad to know."

"*What* don't you want me to know?" Colt's deep voice said.

Kathryn felt his commanding presence before she saw him walk around the other side of the bed. Allie flashed her a silent message of pleading not to give her away.

"About the present I'm getting you for your birthday next week."

Allie's explanation sounded convincing enough,

but Kathryn knew her father didn't believe it for an instant.

"My lips are sealed," Kathryn said to Colt with a playful smile.

"That makes two against one," he teased back without challenging Allie, but his light tone didn't reach his eyes. "I guess I'm going to have to settle for being surprised."

The tension emanating from him made it impossible to stay in the room. "If you two will excuse me, I'm going downstairs to work on that puzzle." Father and daughter needed to be alone. She eyed Allie. "I'll be up in an hour to take your vitals before you go to sleep."

"Okay."

COLT HATED SECRETS. He was glad Katy had chosen to leave the room because he had a few things to say to his daughter in private. After sitting down on the bed next to her, he grasped the hand closest to him. "Your hair looks pretty."

"She brushed it for me."

"Ms. McFarland appears to be an excellent nurse who no doubt will be in high demand for the coming holiday."

"You're wrong about that, Dad."

It looked as if they were going to talk about their guest whether he wanted to or not. "In what way?"

"She doesn't have another patient to take care of on Thanksgiving."

"In other words, she's willing to make herself at home here and at your aunt's, even though she thinks you'll be well enough to be up and around by tomorrow?"

His daughter studied him with a speculative expression. "You don't trust her, do you?" She removed her hand.

Her question jolted him. "We both owe her a debt of gratitude. Why can't you let it go at that?"

Allie didn't look away. "You act like she's taking advantage of us or something."

He breathed in deeply. "Let's put it this way. Even if the patient advocacy program provides this service, she's done something unprecedented by bringing you home. It's possible that now she's had a good look around, Ms. McFarland is a shrewd enough woman to play on your emotions hoping to extend her stay and see where it all leads."

Her eyes never left his. "I knew that was why you didn't like her, but Katy's not looking for a rich husband," she assured him.

He eyed her with incredulity. "Why would you say something like that?"

"I happened to overhear Michelle's mom on the phone to one of her friends. She said that with your looks and money, you would always be a woman magnet and that's probably why you haven't remarried yet."

Somehow when Colt wasn't watching, Allie had become an adult. His precocious fifteen-year-old daughter had thrown the gloves away. He didn't know her like this. "Allie—"

"I'll prove that you're wrong about Katy."

To his surprise she slid out the other side of the bed and walked to her closet. He saw her pull something out of her parka pocket. She scuttled back under the covers and handed him a brochure, of all things. "Here, Dad. Read this."

Colt had no idea what he thought he was going to see when he looked down at it. The picture staring back at him resembled the woman downstairs. He read the words beneath it.

Kathryn McFarland, lost for twenty-six years, has been FOUND!

McFarland... Suddenly it all came rushing back to him. The famous Utah kidnapping case involving the Copper King's family, whose wealth rivaled that of the Vanderbilts and the Carnegies.

He jumped to his feet.

Four years earlier there'd been breaking news on every television and radio station in America about the baby daughter stolen from four-time U.S. Senator Reed McFarland and his wife. After twenty-six years, she'd been found and was now back with her family.

Some newscasters had said the case was bigger, yet gruesomely similar to the Lindbergh kidnapping back in 1932 when the baby was stolen out of their home, but the McFarlands' story had a happy ending.

Katy was *that* Kathryn?

He stared at the picture again.

"That's the photo the FBI first released to the press. It was taken while she was still living at Skwars Farm."

Colt thought she looked like a deer caught in the headlights. Four years had wrought changes. She had a longer hairstyle now and a polish lacking in the photograph, but the facial features and beautiful bone structure couldn't be denied. When he tore his eyes from her picture, he read the information from front to back.

"That brochure only tells you about the foundation, Dad. Besides running it, you ought to hear all the other things she and her family do to help people."

For the next few minutes, he listened while Allie proceeded to enlighten him on the extraordinary way she'd carried on with her life since being reunited with her family. Each new revelation made him more shameful of his cynicism.

The McFarlands had lived through the horror of waking up to find their baby missing from her crib. Colt's panic when he'd first learned Allie had gone off and no one knew where she was had given him a small taste of their terror.

He reflected on Ms. McFarland's phone call to him and could only praise her for the calm way she'd let Colt know Allie was all right. That was because she knew how to talk to frantic parents.

She was no ordinary woman. Colt couldn't compare her to the other women he'd known over the years. In all fairness, probably some of them hadn't been out for all they could get from him, but he'd never let those relationships last long enough to prove him wrong. Allie hadn't been completely off in her assessment.

He rubbed the back of his neck, experiencing a new level of panic. All he had to do was look at his daughter. The telltale stars in her eyes when she talked about Katy bordered on hero worship. Allie could have searched the world over and not have found a more heroic person to idolize than the nurse who'd accompanied her to Bozeman.

Ms. McFarland needed to get back to her life. They needed to get back to theirs. Once Allie was better and

Colt was alone with his daughter again, he would con-
front her. He suspected why she'd gone to Salt Lake
without telling him, but needed to hear it from her.
When everything was out in the open and he could tell
her he understood her reasons, then their lives could
return to normal.

He handed Allie the brochure. "Keep this for your
scrapbook. When you're old, you'll be able to tell your
grandchildren that you were once taken care of by one
of the most famous women in America, certainly the
most altruistic."

"Altruistic? I never heard that word before."

"It means unselfish concern for the welfare of
others. The McFarlands could have invented the
word," he murmured. "We've encroached on her generosity long enough. She needs to get back to her other
responsibilities."

"When is she leaving?" Allie cried out.

"If your temperature returns to normal by tomorrow,
then I'll drive her to the airport." That was a given. If
Allie's temperature shot up again, he'd ask Dr. Rawson
to make a house call.

"But she said a couple of days—"

"Today and tomorrow represent a couple of days,
honey. I'm going downstairs to do some work. I would
imagine she'll be up soon to get you ready for bed. I'll
peek in on you later to kiss you good night."

Her crushed expression was the last thing he saw
before he almost bumped into Matt coming up the stairs.
"Hey—where are you going so fast?"

"I'm getting the DVD they passed out at the football
banquet from my room. Katy wants to watch it."

"Maybe you could visit your sister for a little while first? If we take turns, she won't be so bored."

Matt got that impatient look on his face, but he muttered, "Okay."

"Thanks. Who knows? Before long it might be you lying in bed with the flu, wishing someone would keep you company."

Colt found their guest seated on the couch in the great room. She was watching the national news while she talked to someone on her cell phone.

Illuminated by the fire, she made a riveting picture, Before her glance flicked to his, he'd picked up on the serious tone of her conversation. While he waited for her to hang up, he wandered over to the puzzle and fit in some pieces.

KATHRYN HAD EXPECTED MATT to come back into the room. The sight of his dark-haired father prompted her to tell her sister that unless something changed with Allie, she'd see her at the airport at noon tomorrow. She hung up and turned off the TV.

"Forgive me for ignoring you, Colt."

He looked across at her with his keen gaze. "You didn't have to do that for me."

No, but he'd brought a restless energy into the room that put her on edge. "There wasn't anything of interest to watch. I'm glad you came in so I could talk to you before I go upstairs. When you walked in on Allie and me earlier, she'd just told me something in confidence.

"For the sake of not upsetting her, I went along with her excuse about your birthday present. But I'm going up now to say good night to her. When I do, I'll tell her she mustn't keep secrets from you. Not that she needs any encouragement from me. She loves you too terribly to hold back much longer. What I'm hoping is that it will be sooner than later so you can have some peace. Good night."

More convinced than ever that he was only putting up with her presence for Allie's sake, she left the family room, anxious to separate herself from him. He probably wasn't aware he had that effect on her. The man was in hell with good reason.

Kathryn was so immersed in her troubled thoughts, she almost bumped into Matt at the top of the stairs with a DVD in his hand. She'd forgotten about that.

He slowed down. "I was just coming, but I had to talk to Allie first."

"Of course. Your sister has top priority." She looked at her watch. "I didn't realize how late it was getting and decided I'd better get my patient ready for bed. Tell you what. Leave the DVD downstairs and we'll watch it together in the morning. I really do want to see it." If his father hadn't been down there, she wouldn't have come up yet.

"Sure."

She felt his trail of disappointment as she went to her room to get her bag. Kathryn didn't like that her presence seemed to be creating a disturbance in Colt's household.

When she walked into Allie's room a moment later, the teen was listening to her iPod. She raised a sad face to Kathryn before removing the headset. "Hi."

"Hi, yourself. Looks like your brother's been taking care of you. That's nice."

Allie didn't say anything. "Let's check that temperature first."

After the beep went off, Kathryn checked the numbers. "Ninety-eight point eight. That's in the normal range. Tomorrow you'll be able to get dressed and go downstairs." She checked her lungs and blood pressure. Everything looked good.

"You're going home tomorrow, huh?"

Her mournful tone didn't escape Kathryn. She put everything back in her bag. "Unless you take a turn for the worse, which I don't believe will happen." She handed her a glass of water and the pills.

Tears glazed her brown eyes as she swallowed them. "Have you decided you can't help me find my mom?"

Kathryn had been expecting that question. "There's no such thing as *can't,* Allie, but this is something you have to discuss with your father. I wouldn't dream of going behind his back to help you with something so painful and private for both of you. He's been such a wonderful father to you all these years, he deserves to know what you're thinking and feeling."

Allie bit her lip. "What if he gets mad at me?"

"You were grown up enough to go to Salt Lake on your own. At this point he realizes you're no longer a child incapable of relating to adult problems. Give him a chance and he'll surprise you with his understanding."

"You think?" Her eyes had fastened on Kathryn, she wanted to believe her.

"I *know.*" Kathryn couldn't say that about many things, but she'd felt Colt's deep love for Allie. So deep, in fact, she had an idea he was still in shock over what his daughter had done.

"Can I call you after you get back to Salt Lake? I'll use the phone number printed on the brochure."

Kathryn had to hang tough on this one. "Not unless you have his permission. You want to keep your father's trust, don't you?"

Allie's head was bowed. "Yes."

"So do I. You're very blessed to have a dad like him. I'll see you in the morning. Good night." She fought the impulse to hug her. Kathryn's strong compulsion to give in to Allie's wishes proved that this girl already meant more to her than she should.

After preparing for bed, she reached for her phone and got under the covers to call Donna. There was still no word on the abducted girl. Once they'd hung up, she phoned her parents and learned that her mother had been in contact with the missing girl's family.

The three of them commiserated over the tragic situation. Before she hung up, she told them that if she flew home tomorrow as planned, she expected them to come to her condo for dinner. They were always waiting on other people. Kathryn felt like waiting on them for a change.

This experience with Allie had made her more emotional than usual. Before falling asleep, she prayed that the little kidnapped girl would be found alive and that Allie would find the courage to confide in her father. She eventually fell asleep remembering the joy in Colt's voice and expression as he'd picked up his daughter and carried her to the car. Every parent should have such a happy reunion.

At eight the next morning, Kathryn showered and got ready for the day. She'd packed an oyster-colored silk blouse and dove-gray pants in fine wool, cinched with a wide leather belt. She caught her hair back with a tortoise shell clip and put pearl studs in her ears.

In a minute, she knocked on Allie's door and announced herself.

"Come in." The teen had already showered and looked terrific in a long-sleeved, navy-blue cotton pullover teamed with Levi's and sneakers.

"Well, look at you. I don't think I need to take your vitals, but I'm going to anyway."

"First will you do my hair like you wore yours yesterday?" Allie handed her the brush.

"Of course. Have you got a scarf?"

"No, but will this neckerchief do?"

"Let me see it."

Allie pulled it out of her middle drawer. It was a Levi brand with a navy cowboy motif. She handed it to Kathryn.

"I think it's long enough to tie in a bow."

Kathryn brushed her hair back and made short work of it. She studied the teen. Whoever her mother was had to have been a beautiful woman. "You look lovely."

"Thanks."

"Now if you'll indulge me while I check you, then we can go downstairs for breakfast." A couple of minutes later and it was all over. "Your temperature is normal, Allie."

"That's what I was afraid of," she mumbled.

"You don't really mean that," Kathryn said, trying to be cheerful. "Although you still have some head

congestion, your lungs are clear. Just take it easy for
another day or two to get back your strength. Take your
pills now, then we'll go."

"Okay."

Once that was accomplished, they left the bedroom
and walked toward the staircase. Colt was coming up
the steps two at a time, dressed in a plaid flannel shirt
in reds and blues. He wore Levi's and cowboy boots.

By accident, his eyes lifted to Kathryn's, forcing her
to swallow the cry in her throat. Beneath his inky-black
hair and brows, those orbs had taken on the color of
crystal green shards.

"Good morning, Ms. McFarland."

Kathryn found him the most attractive man she'd ever
met in her life. "Good morning," she answered back,
thankful she could speak.

Until she'd flown in yesterday, her brother-in-law
Jake Halsey had been the only living male to merit that
distinction. Considine lurked in her dreams. Who knew
the day would come when a forbidding Montana cowboy
who jealously guarded his mountain isolation would
topple them both in an instant.

He switched his attention to Allie. "Hi, honey. Noreen
has breakfast on the table. I was just coming up to get
you. I guess I don't have to ask how you're feeling."

"Her temperature is normal," Kathryn volunteered
when Allie only muttered something indistinct.

"That's the best news yet." He reached for her and
carried her the rest of the way.

"Dad, put me down. I'm not a baby." But she said it
with a giggle.

"Don't you know you'll always be my baby girl?" he teased before setting her on her feet with another hug.

When Kathryn imagined him hugging her like that, a shiver of delight raced through her body. She followed father and daughter through to the other side of their home, not having seen the vaulted living and dining room before. The same refined rustic decor and tall windows ran through the entire house.

So much daylight opened up the rooms to nature. The sight of new fallen snow from the night before was glorious. She almost blurted that this had to be one of the most beautiful spots on Earth, but she caught herself in time.

While Colt helped her and Allie to the table laden with scones and bacon, Matt came running in wearing a polo and jeans. He flashed Kathryn a smile before taking a seat next to their father. "I was hoping you guys would be up."

"After we eat, I want to see your video, Matt."

"Which one is that?" Allie wanted to know.

"My football banquet DVD."

Kathryn turned to her. "Have you seen it?"

Allie rolled her eyes. "About a dozen times."

"Then it must be good."

"Except we lost in the playoffs," he said.

"That doesn't matter, Matt. To think your team made it that far is terrific. Not every guy has the ability or the opportunity to even go out for football. Someday, you'll be able to show it to your children. Think how fun that will be for you and them."

Colt shot her an enigmatic glance. "Do you have a favorite sport besides football?"

Matt must have told his father what she'd confided to him. "Yes. It's skiing."

"We love it, too, don't we, Dad?"

"We do," he answered.

"Are you really going back to Salt Lake today?"

"Yes. At noon."

"Noon!" Both teens moaned aloud.

"Since your sister is on the mend, I'm needed elsewhere."

"But if you stayed until tomorrow, you could go skiing with us this afternoon."

"Matt! You heard Ms. McFarland. I'll be driving her to the airport shortly. There'll be no skiing for us today. We're staying in with Allie, and you have some home-work to get busy on before school tomorrow."

"Can I at least go with you to take her to the airport?"

Kathryn heard Colt's hesitation before the answer came. "I don't see why not. Noreen will be here to keep an eye on Allie."

"I don't need her to watch me." His daughter's pre-dictable response settled things for Kathryn.

Not wanting to get in the middle of a talk with his disgruntled children, she got up from the table. "Those scones were fabulous. Excuse me for a minute while I go in the kitchen and thank Noreen. Then I'll watch your video."

Colt wanted to see the back of Kathryn. She was doing her best to oblige him. Only another hour before he drove her to the airport and out of their lives.

Chapter Five

The snow had been heavier on the mountain, but last night's storm hadn't developed into anything ferocious. By the time Colt turned his car onto the highway, the plows had already been out to clear it for the rest of the drive into Bozeman. The clouds had opened up, allowing the sun to shine through.

Under normal circumstances, it was his favorite kind of winter day, but today had a different feel about it. An intangible gloom had descended over his household and none of his efforts could shake it. He'd left Allie seated in front of the fire to work on the puzzle with Ed. Between her red-rimmed eyes and his broken arm, they made quite a pair.

When Matt had brought Ms. McFarland's suitcase down to the Xterra, she'd moved ahead of him and had climbed in the backseat. His son got in front with him. So far Colt hadn't looked in the rearview mirror. He didn't want to meet a pair of blue eyes and be electrified by them again. It had happened with every chance glance since yesterday.

Matt turned his head toward her. "Katy? Are you going to the Utah-BYU football game on Saturday?"

"It's possible, especially because they'll be playing at the U, which is five minutes away from me. But I might have to work."

"Rich and I are going skiing, so I'm going to record it and then watch it after. Maybe I'll see you on TV."

She chuckled. "I'll probably end up having to tape it, too. I'm hoping we win. Last year we lost in overtime and it about killed everybody."

Colt listened while they talked about the flaws and virtues of both teams' quarterbacks. Once they passed the airport security check, he obtained permission to drive on through to the area where the white Cessna was parked on the tarmac.

"There's my ride. Have to run so I don't hold them up." She opened the back door and got out so fast with her suitcase, neither he nor Matt had time to assist her.

She eyed them without really looking at them, then smiled. "It's been a pleasure meeting Allie's family. Thank you for your hospitality. I won't forget." She extended her gloved hand, which they both shook. "Tell her to stay well, now."

Colt nodded, finally allowing himself to take in the sight of her shapely figure clad in the white parka. "I hope you know how indebted I am to you."

"I *do* know."

Yes, she did. The found Kathryn McFarland knew it better than most anyone else in the world.

"If I get sick, will you come and nurse me?"

Gentle laughter escaped her throat. "You've got a whole wonderful family to help you, Matt. Just take care you don't break a leg skiing on Saturday or you'll let your wrestling coach down."

He grinned. "You don't have to worry about me."

Still clutching her suitcase, she turned and started toward the open door of the plane. Colt watched her disappear inside. Disturbed by the odd sensation that swept through him, he wheeled around and strode back to his car. The second Matt got in, Colt started the motor and they took off.

On the way out of the airport he saw the Cessna gaining altitude. As it changed to a speck before vanishing from sight, he could suddenly put words to what was going on inside him.

Hell, hell and hell...

"Dad? Are you okay?"

Trust Matt's radar to detect the slightest irregularity. "Of course. Why do you ask?"

He hunched his shoulders. "I don't know. You've been acting kind of weird since Katy brought Allie home."

Colt drew in his breath. "That's because your sister has a lot of explaining to do. Now that Katy's gone, I'm going to get to the bottom of Allie's disappearing act."

Katy had taken his daughter's secret with her. Though he admired her integrity, he wished he hadn't been such a bad parent, that Allie didn't feel comfortable approaching him rather than turning to a stranger. Colt accepted total responsibility for this impasse. By a strange twist of circumstance, Ms. McFarland's unexpected intervention during Allie's crisis had underlined his need to deal with this problem head-on before the day was out.

"Are you mad?"

He made a gruff sound in his throat. What a question! Yes, he was mad, but not for the reasons his son was no doubt entertaining. "Let's just say she gave us both a scare I never want to live through again."

"Me, neither. What she did was *crazy*."

"Not to her." Not to her.

"Katy was totally cool."

High praise, coming from his son. "I agree." To say anything more would encourage him. He didn't want to talk about her.

Colt turned at the entrance to the ranch where his tire tracks were still noticeable in the snow. They began the climb to the house.

"As soon as we get back, is it okay if I take Blackie on a short run? I want to see how his leg is doing now."

"Go ahead." Nothing like a ride to put life back into perspective.

Colt walked into the house expecting to find Allie in the living room, but Noreen told him she was in her bedroom on the phone. If he didn't miss his guess, she'd called Jen. "She's pretty broken up about Katy leaving."

Tell me something else I don't know, Noreen. "As long as I'm free for the moment, I might as well tackle the disposal." Anything to get his mind off the woman he'd thought of as Kathryn from the moment he'd read her full name on the brochure. He knew he hadn't liked the shortened version. It didn't suit her.

"Then I'll leave you to it. If you need me, I'll be at the other house."

"Thanks for all you do, Noreen."

Half an hour later, he'd finished the job and was

washing his hands when his cell phone rang. It was the bus depot telling him Allie's backpack had just been brought in on the bus from Salt Lake. He thanked them and let them know he'd be by for it later.

In case Allie was thirsty for something besides water, he grabbed a couple of colas out of the fridge and headed up to her room. He knocked on the door. "It's your dad."

"Come in," she answered in a flat voice.

He opened the door and found her sprawled on her stomach across the top of her bed with her shoes off and the phone in hand. She peered up at him with a crestfallen expression. "Is Katy gone?"

"Yes. By now she's been back in Salt Lake for a while." He moved a chair over to the side of the bed and sat down. "I brought you a drink."

"Thanks." She sat up cross-legged and took it from him. They both opened the tabs and drank. Colt liked the way Kathryn had done her hair with the neck scarf. "I apologized to Jen and her parents," she volunteered.

"That's good." After finishing off half the can, he put it on the floor. When he looked up, her eyes were swimming in tears.

"I'm sorry for what I did, Dad. I mean…about everything."

"Honey." He took her can from her and put it on the floor next to his. "I've the gut feeling this has to do with your mother, so before this talk goes any further, I want you to know I take full blame for what happened. This *is* about your mother, right?"

She nodded before burying her face in her hands.

"Dad?" Matt's voice sounded from the hallway.

"In your sister's room!" he called back. "Come on in."

Matt stood in the doorway staring at the two of them. "What's going on?"

"As I just told Allie, it's my fault she went to Salt Lake without telling anyone. It's time the three of us had the conversation I should have had with you years ago. Pull up the other chair."

He saw his twins exchange a private glance before Matt did his bidding.

"I've already told you my parents froze to death during a blizzard when I was four and your aunt Sherry was six. They didn't marry until their mid-thirties, so we came along late in their lives.

"What's interesting is that my grandfather didn't meet my grandmother until they were in their thirties. My father was their only child and he wasn't born until my grandmother was forty. I'm telling you all this because I was the dark horse in the Brenner family. I got married at twenty and had you two right off the bat." They both laughed.

"My grandparents loved you like you were their own children. They helped me raise you. I wish you could remember them, but you were too little when they passed away within a year of each other. I can tell you this much." Emotion almost closed his throat. "They were saints."

He eyed them with an ache in his heart because he was about to break his silence. When they heard the unvarnished truth, it would shatter them. His grandmother had warned him to tell them everything when they were old enough to understand, but for fear of hurting his children, he'd waited years too long. Now all three of them were going to be in a new kind of pain.

ON SATURDAY MORNING, Kathryn finished checking on one of the children at Renaissance House who needed to see a dentist, then went downstairs to make the appointment. When that was done, she let herself into her brother's office. While she waited for him to get off the phone, she wandered over to the windows overlooking the snow-dusted east gardens of the estate. The grounds became a fairyland of flowers in every season but winter.

It was cold out there this morning. Beneath an overcast sky, everything looked dead. Her thoughts flew to the Cloud Bottom Ranch, as she liked to think of it. Winter clothed the pines in a grandeur of pristine white.

Colt, astride his stallion, would be up on the mountain checking the herds. She could see the lone, tall cowboy in silhouette. He would be dressed in sheepskin and a cowboy hat covering midnight-black hair while he looked over his empire, making sure everything was in working order. His hard-boned feat—

"Yoo-hoo! Kathryn?" When she realized her brother was talking to her, she turned around, flush-faced. "Where were you?" he teased with a smile.

"I was wondering if it's going to snow before the football game this afternoon."

His blue eyes searched hers. "I don't think that was the only thing on your mind. You've been different since you got back from Montana. Everyone at Thanksgiving dinner noticed it."

She averted her gaze. "It's because that little girl hasn't been found yet."

"That and something else." Cord was psychic. "Whenever you want to talk about it, I'm your man."

"You think I don't know that?"

"Just checking. Are you going to the game with all of us?"

"That depends on what's happening at the foundation." She walked over to his closet for her parka and put it on. "I'm heading there now. If more volunteers are needed to continue the search, I'll be manning the phone."

"I'll save a seat for you in case you come late."

"Thanks."

"Do you know you work too hard? All the signs are there."

She leaned over the desk to peck his cheek without saying anything before leaving the mansion through the south entrance. The plaza was only a block down the street. Except for a few frozen spots, she accomplished her short jaunt on mostly dry pavement.

A group of people surrounded the "Blessed are the Children" sculpture that stood in the courtyard. She hurried past them to enter the doors and immediately heard the recording, "Welcome to the Kathryn McFarland Foundation. Take the time to come in and learn how to help us fight crime so the next kidnapping won't be your child."

Walking past the lobby screens showing the dates and times of the latest kidnap victims, Kathryn headed for the front desk. She could see several of the staff huddled together.

"What's going on?"

One of the new volunteer recruits named Melanie turned to her. "I was just going to phone you. We heard from a team of rescuers. They came across a little girl's unclothed remains up Millcreek Canyon."

A moan broke from Kathryn. It could be Whitney, but no one would know until the forensic expert got busy. Whatever the answer, someone's dear little child had been murdered.

"I'm going to my condo and calling home. My parents need to know what we've learned." They would want to be there for Whitney's family and wait for the news with them. "I'll be back."

"But I thought this was your day off."

"I don't always take one." Kathryn would rather be here. She was too restless. Work kept her from thinking. "See you in a while."

She walked out to the lobby and headed for the bank of elevators servicing the plaza tower. She took the private lift used exclusively for the penthouse. Only Kathryn and her family knew the code.

As soon as she walked into the living room, she removed her parka and sat down on the couch to phone her parents. As she knew they would, once she'd given them the update, they called off their plans to attend the game. No one could enjoy it right now.

After she hung up, she set the HD/DVR to record it. She'd left the condo without eating breakfast and knew she needed nourishment, but the news about a little girl's remains having been discovered hit her like a body slam. Her appetite was nonexistent.

Those poor parents.

Every time there was a watch-and-wait period, she thought about her own parents' agony of thirty years ago and got sick inside. Kathryn had assumed that after running the foundation since her graduation, she wouldn't react like this, but if anything her response to each new tragedy seemed to be affecting her more adversely than ever.

Her parents were so strong! Kathryn wasn't anything like them and would never be able to measure up. That distressed her so terribly she couldn't stand her own company. She freshened up, eager to get back to work. Working kept the demons at bay.

On her way through the living room for her purse, her cell rang, causing her stomach to clench. Kathryn didn't think it possible the child's body could be identified this quickly, but a comparison of dental records might have already been done.

She pulled out her phone and glanced at the caller ID. "Hi, Melanie. Has there been official word yet?"

"No." In a hushed voice she said, "I'm calling because this gorgeous—and I mean *gorgeous as in the extreme*—guy came over to the desk asking for you. I told him to stroll around and look at the exhibits while I tried to reach you."

Only one male on Earth fit that description, but he didn't venture outside his mountain kingdom unless it was a dire emergency.

Since Melanie was a twenty-year-old college student working for them part-time and a natural flirt, Kathryn could forgive her for the over-the-top exaggeration. "What's his name?"

"He said to tell you he was from the Circle B, but if you weren't available, he'd be back later."

Kathryn clutched the phone against her chest, hardly able to breathe. When she could find the words she said, "Tell him to wait for me. I'll be right down." She clicked off before Melanie could ask questions Kathryn had no intention of answering.

Right now her curiosity was on the verge of exploding, but she didn't have time to ponder his reason for being here. The fact that he knew where to come looking for her meant he'd talked in-depth with his daughter. All Kathryn could do was fly to the bedroom and change out of the work clothes she'd worn to Renaissance House.

Colt had only seen her in pants, so she donned a three-piece Pendleton wool suit in rich plum and slipped on her black dolly-pointed kidskin pumps. She put gold studs in her ears, then ran a brush through her hair. It had a natural wave and hung loose from a side part. A light spray of Fleurs d'Elle mist and she was ready. For *what* exactly she didn't know.

Maybe he'd brought the twins with him. Her pulse raced all the way to the plaza foyer. At the moment the only thing that mattered to her was that he'd either flown or driven to Salt Lake and had sought her out.

Slow down, Kathryn. Walk, don't run to him.

Reflecting back to her mid-teens, she'd always been the one to run from men who wanted a relationship with her. Yet a relationship was the last thing Colton Brenner had on his mind. He hadn't come here to pursue her. Far from it.

Your fantasizing days are over. Remember?

By the time she entered her workplace, she'd come to

her senses and could handle the sight of him standing at the counter, being chatted up by her staff. In his Stetson and black bomber jacket, every eye in the room, male or female, was riveted on him.

Gorgeous in the extreme, Melanie had said because there were no words, in any language, that came close to truly defining him.

She knew the moment he saw her. His head reared back like a Thoroughbred stallion's. He stepped away from the counter and started his long-legged stride toward her. As she saw him in the flesh once more, an unbidden thrill of excitement went through her.

"Hello, Colt." She rejoiced that her voice sounded so steady.

"Kathryn," he murmured. Not Katy. That meant he'd read her full name in the brochure and had chosen to use it.

Taking the initiative, she extended her hand. It got lost in his strong one.

"I hoped we might meet again one day, but didn't expect it to be this soon." She searched the green gaze focused on her. "Is Allie all right? Matt?"

"That depends on your definition of all right." His deep voice rumbled through her before he let go. "If you're talking about her physical condition, she's quite well thanks to you. So far, Matt hasn't come down with the flu." His eyes unexpectedly glinted in amusement, making him irresistible.

Her mouth went dry. "Did you come to Salt Lake alone?"

He nodded. "I flew in a little while ago and took a

taxi here hoping to catch you before you left for the football game with your family."

"I—I'm not going," she stammered.

"Why not?"

"I'll show you." She walked over to the screen with Whitney's picture. "This little girl has been missing for a week. Early this morning, a body was found up one of the canyons. My parents have gone to be with the girl's family while they await word from the police."

She tried to swallow, but the lump in her throat made it close to impossible. "This is a very hard time for everyone associated with the foundation."

"I think it must be hardest on you."

The compassion in his eyes drove her to avert her head. He'd managed to zero in on the troubling thoughts she'd been entertaining earlier. "How long are you planning to be here, Colt?"

"As long as it takes to talk to you, but obviously this isn't a good time."

To leave his children, she had to assume he wanted something specific from her.

"While we're in waiting mode, this is probably the best time. Have you eaten yet?"

"I had breakfast with the kids before I left."

"That was several hours ago. Come to my condo and I'll feed you while you tell me what's on your mind. It's just across the lobby in the tower. If I'm needed, one of the girls at the desk will phone me."

He studied her for a moment. "I don't believe you have a selfish bone in your body."

"That's because you don't know me."

They dodged a crowd of people shopping for Christmas and took the elevator to the penthouse. During the short ride, the warmth from his powerful body seeped into hers. She could smell the scent of the soap he'd used in the shower. Her awareness of him was so potent, it unnerved her.

When the door opened and she stepped into the foyer, she breathed more easily. "If you'll give me your coat, I'll hang it in the closet."

Colt shrugged out of his jacket, then removed his hat and put it on the hall table.

She walked him through the elegant living room with its more traditional décor. "I'm sure you'd like to freshen up. Go down that hall. The guest bathroom is the first door on your left. When you want to find me, I'll be in the kitchen. It's beyond the dining room you can see from here."

"Thank you. I'll try not to get lost," he said in a wry tone.

Kathryn had cooked for Steve several times, but early on she'd realized her feelings for him tended to be sisterly. She'd never known the kind of excitement Colt engendered simply by being in the same room with him.

After washing her hands, she got busy frying bacon for the club sandwiches. He'd probably like soup and a salad, too. When he walked in and lounged against the wall looking fantastic in a white polo and jeans, she almost cut her finger while she was slicing the tomatoes.

"What can I do to help?"

She finished tossing the salad. "If you'll take the

plates into the dining room, I'll bring the coffee." Kathryn discovered she had an appetite after all.

"The view's incredible from up here," he said once they'd sat down at the table to eat. "Quite a change from Skwars Farm, Wisconsin." On that note, he devoured three quarters of his sandwich in one go while she ate her soup.

"Allie must have an excellent memory to recall that detail."

He eyed her over the rim of his coffee cup. "After being mesmerized by your extraordinary story, she wasn't bound to forget such an unusual name. The food's delicious, by the way."

"Thank you."

"I remember when you were found."

Reminding her of that day changed the tone of their conversation. "Even up on your mountain?"

Colt finished off the last of his sandwich. "News like that has long legs."

"I remember that day, too," she teased in order not to break down. There were two kinds of *found*. Whitney's unknown fate haunted her.

"It was a stunning development, the kind no one could believe. I'll be honest and tell you that since Allie showed me the brochure, I've been incredulous she would have ended up being the recipient of Kathryn McFarland's exceptional kindness. What are the odds of that happening?"

"Probably as great as the odds of your lovely daughter getting on a bus to come to Salt Lake one dark winter night without your knowledge."

His gaze sobered as it wandered over her features.

"What prompted you to take the time out from your heavy workload to accompany Allie all the way to Montana? If you performed that kind of service for everyone who needed help, there'd be nothing left of you."

Once again, Colt had asked a question that hit at the core of her growing distress. "I could say that your daughter is an exceptional girl and a real charmer. Both descriptions are true. But now that you've prompted me to think about it, I have to admit I was driven by an underlying anger."

He stopped munching on his salad. "Anger?"

Without realizing it, she'd crushed the paper napkin in her fist. "I have a lot of it inside me, Colt. When I first saw Allie lying there and went through her clothes looking for clues, I could see she came from a wonderful home. Everything about her screamed excellent health. She was well cared for."

Kathryn warmed to her subject. "It was obvious she'd been given every advantage in life. Once she spoke to me, she displayed good manners. In fact, she was so different from most of the troubled teens who end up at Renaissance House, I wanted to shake her for causing the most wonderful father in the world in her opinion so much grief. I knew you had to be in hell."

Their eyes met in silent understanding. To her chagrin, her lids began to prickle as emotion swamped her. "At her age I would have given anything on Earth to know my parents and swore that if I were ever united with them, I'd never leave their sight.

"I'd been told that my great-aunt Marie Buric had brought me to Skwars Farm because her grandson and his wife had abandoned me. After she died, her daughter

Olga took care of me until she died. From then on I was passed around the farming families. For years I prayed my parents would come and get me. I had no idea I'd been kidnapped by strangers and my real parents were looking for me. To have a home, an identity—you can't imagine what it's like not to have those things. But getting back to your question, I suppose a part of me felt compelled to see Allie home safely and *make* her realize how blessed she was to belong to you."

Colt's hand covered her fist clutching the napkin. "Thank God for you, Kathryn." His heartfelt touch filled her with warmth.

"Thank my remarkable parents." She put her other hand on top of his for a moment and squeezed gently before easing both away. "Their money started the foundation. They gave me this beautiful penthouse, paid my tuition so I could become a nurse. Without the patient advocacy program they set up, I would never have been called in on Allie's case. I'll never be able to repay them for giving me my life." Her voice shook as she spoke.

He sat forward, studying her with eyes so alive and green that she couldn't tear her own gaze away. "Don't you know that being united with their beautiful daughter was all the payment they could ever want? You're not a parent, but I am. Last Friday night when I couldn't find Allie, I had a brief taste of their terror. I never want to go through that again."

"No," she whispered.

"Your honesty has given me deeper insight into my daughter's soul. The powerful emotions that drove you all those years are driving my daughter. Though Matt's not vocal about it, both children need answers about the mother who abandoned them. What worries me is that without them, Allie's going to be stunted in ways I don't want to think about."

Kathryn stared at him. "You can't provide the answers?"

"After I got home from taking you to the airport, I sat down with the twins and told them as much truth as I felt they could handle. It's something I should have done years ago. My grandmother warned me that if I didn't explain things as soon as they could understand, there'd be repercussions."

A shadow darkened his eyes. "Considering Allie's behavior, my grandmother was a prophetess. Too late after the fact, the children now know their mother hated the ranch, hated being under my grandparents' thumb and hated me most of all for taking her away from the money and glitter of big-city life. Unfortunately that explanation isn't enough for Allie. She still wants to find her mother."

"Is that an impossibility?"

"Maybe. Maybe not. The twins were in the hospital a month. She never went in to hold or feed them. When I finally brought them home, she took off for long periods. After they'd been home a week, she went out one day and never returned. I knew she'd planned to leave me, so I can't say I was surprised."

Kathryn groaned. "Allie told me that prior to your marriage Natalie had been raised by her aunt and uncle in Salt Lake. Would she have gone there?"

Colt's eyes turned to flint. "No. During one of our fights, she admitted that her aunt and uncle were a tale of fiction. There was no Beehive Motel, but by that time

I'd figured as much because she never wanted to travel to Salt Lake to see them. It all came out that she'd lived in one foster home after another until she got a job in Las Vegas, where we met."

"Oh, Colt…"

"That's what you get for marrying a woman after only knowing her two weeks."

Two weeks? A stab of pain went through her. Colt had to have been besotted.

"Perhaps now you can understand why early on I maintained the story that she'd grown up in Salt Lake. I couldn't bring myself to tell the children their father's immaturity and poor lack of judgment had doomed them to a motherless existence. When you phoned me, I was horrified to think Allie had gone there on a wild-goose chase."

"It's only natural you wanted to protect them."

"Don't try to make it better, Kathryn, because you can't. I take full responsibility for being too drunk on the rodeo life to pay attention to what was really important until it was too late. The thing that alarms me now is that even though the twins know most of the truth, Allie's still wondering if Natalie might have been the object of foul play. In her mind, that would explain why she never came home that day."

"That's because she's heard *my* story," Kathryn lamented. On top of having been married to an irresponsible child, Colt was in real trouble because he had a daughter who was a big dreamer like Kathryn. Until presented with incontrovertible truth about her mother's character, Allie would cling to the possibility that something terrible had happened to her.

"You're right," Colt muttered. "My daughter would rather believe her mother's alive somewhere, unable to return home to her children rather than accept the alternative. In truth, Natalie tried several times to go in for an abortion, but I caught her in time."

Kathryn froze. "Do the children know about that?"

"No. I hope they never have to know. The fact is, I told Natalie I'd do anything for her if she would carry the babies to term. We made a bargain. I gave her all the savings I had and told her she could leave me after they were born, no questions asked." Colt stopped pacing. "She left with the money all right and made sure she stayed lost."

The revelations kept coming. "Was it a big sum?"

"No, but you don't have to worry about Natalie. She was resourceful. It took a while before I realized she'd stolen the world championship gold buckle I'd won at the NFR in Las Vegas. It was worth at least fifteen thousand dollars at the time. If she found the right buyer, she could have sold it for a great deal more money."

Kathryn got up from the table. "I'll pour us some more hot coffee." She needed a minute alone to absorb what he'd just told her. When she returned to the dining room, she put his cup and saucer in front of him. "I didn't give you cream or sugar, but maybe I should have asked the first time."

"As you figured out last week, I like it black."

"Having been raised on a farm, I learned to drink it with a lot of both. It's a habit I can't seem to break."

"We all need one or two of life's little pleasures to keep us going."

"I'm a chocolaholic, too," she confessed.

One corner of his compelling mouth lifted. "Aren't we all?" After he took a big swallow of the steaming liquid, he set the cup down. "How did your sister trace you to Wisconsin?"

His question told her exactly why he'd flown to Salt Lake. It didn't come as a shock, but she suffered the pang of disappointment to realize that where she was concerned, there was nothing personal about this visit.

She cleared her throat. "Maggie had the help of an undercover CIA agent named Jake Halsey who eventually became her husband. She'd gone to a genealogical firm hoping someone could research the name Buric. It was the only lead my family had to go on. Jake started working on it and cracked the case."

"Is he still with the CIA?"

"He has all the connections, but now that they're married and have a little boy, he works as a genealogist and gives the bureau help on certain difficult cases."

Her guest studied her for a moment. "I'd like to hire your brother-in-law to find Natalie. I'll pay any fee he charges."

"If he can do it, you couldn't find a better man for the job." She checked her watch. "I'm pretty sure he's already left for the game. Tell you what. If you're going to fly back today, I'll talk to him this evening and ask him to call you. Would that be all right?"

"I couldn't ask for more."

Gone in an instant was the hope that he'd be staying overnight in Salt Lake. Her spirits sank to another level.

He finished his coffee. "I know your coworkers are

waiting downstairs for you, so I'll leave and let you get back to your vigil. For what it's worth, I'm torn up over the little girl's kidnapping. At least if it's her body they found, the parents will be able to have a proper burial for her and try to cope with their loss."

She saw a glint of pain in his eyes before he added, "Unlike your family, who must have suffered hundreds of little deaths each time a body was found that might have been yours and then wasn't. Because of my own joy hearing from you that Allie was all right, I have some appreciation for your parents' joy when you were found."

Colt understood a lot.

"That was one incredible day." Kathryn put on a bright smile, pretending that his plan to fly back to Montana hadn't affected her. "Let me call for the limo to take you to the airport, then I'll go down in the elevator with you."

Chapter Six

Colt stomped the snow off his boots and entered the ranch house with Allie's backpack. He'd picked it up at the depot on his way home from the airport. Once he'd hung it on a peg, he removed his jacket and hat, before starting down the back hall. "Hello! I'm home!" he called out. "Doesn't anyone care?"

Noreen came in the great room. "I do, but I'm afraid Matt's still with Rich. The Carlisles are bringing Allie home from ice skating."

"It's looks like I got away with flying to Salt Lake undetected." He had no secrets from Noreen and Ed. After all these years, they were part of the family.

She flashed him a conspiratorial smile. "So far so good. I think they've been just as busy making plans for your birthday on Monday. Were you able to meet with Katy?"

Yes, he'd spent time with Kathryn McFarland, and it had gone by in such a flash he might have dreamed it. The last thing he'd wanted to do was leave her condo. If she hadn't been so consumed by her pain over the missing child, he would have planned to stay in Salt Lake overnight and ask her to dinner in order to be with her longer.

But it was just as well things had turned out the way they did. To spend more time with her would be a painful lesson in futility. They lived in different states, led different lives. She belonged to an extraordinary family and would never leave them or abandon her mission.

How to explain that to Matt and Allie who had a crush on her and could be hurt if he didn't squelch their burgeoning feelings for a woman who was already bigger than life to them?

That was why he'd flown to Salt Lake without telling them. If Jake Halsey could help him find Natalie, then progress would have been made without bringing Kathryn into the picture any more than was absolutely necessary.

"I not only met her, she fixed me an amazing lunch on no notice at all. Her penthouse overlooks the Great Salt Lake Valley in every direction. It's pretty spectacular."

"The McFarlands live spectacular lives."

Too spectacular. "Amen to that. I found out her brother-in-law traced her to Wisconsin and broke the case. He's former CIA. Hopefully he'll be able to track Natalie down. Kathryn's going to call me tonight and let me know one way or the other. If he can't do it, then I've got to find someone who can."

"That's got me worried, Colt. There's an old saying about being careful for what you wish for. You might get it."

Lines marred his features. "You try telling that to Allie."

Get 2 Books FREE!

Harlequin® Books,
publisher of women's fiction,
presents

GET 2 BOOKS

We'd like to send you two *Harlequin American Romance®* novels absolutely free! Accepting them puts you under no obligation to purchase any more books.

HOW TO GET YOUR
2 FREE BOOKS AND 2 FREE GIFTS

1. Return the reply card today, and we'll send you two *Harlequin American Romance* novels, absolutely free! We'll even pay the postage!

2. Accepting free books places you under no obligation to buy anything, ever. Whatever you decide, the free books and gifts are yours to keep, free!

3. We hope that after receiving your free books you'll want to remain a subscriber, but the choice is yours—to continue or cancel, any time at all!

EXTRA BONUS

You'll also get two free mystery gifts! (worth about $10)

FREE!

The Reader Service - Here's how it works:

Accepting your 2 free books and 2 free mystery gifts (mystery gifts worth approximately $10.00) places you under no obligation to buy anything. You may keep the books and gifts and return the shipping statement marked "cancel". If you do not cancel, about a month later we'll send you 4 additional books and bill you just $4.24 each in the U.S. or $4.99 each in Canada. That is a savings of at least 15% off the cover price. It's quite a bargain! Shipping and handling is just 50¢ per book.* You may cancel at any time, but if you choose to continue, every month we'll send you 4 more books, which you may either purchase at the discount price or return to us and cancel your subscription.

*Terms and prices subject to change without notice. Prices do not include applicable taxes. Sales tax applicable in N.Y. Canadian residents will be charged GST. Offer not valid in Quebec. Credit or debit balances in a customer's account(s) may be offset by any other outstanding balance owed by or to the customer. Books received may not be as shown.

BUSINESS REPLY MAIL
FIRST-CLASS MAIL   PERMIT NO. 717   BUFFALO, NY

POSTAGE WILL BE PAID BY ADDRESSEE

THE READER SERVICE
PO BOX 1867
BUFFALO NY 14240-9952

NO POSTAGE
NECESSARY
IF MAILED
IN THE
UNITED STATES

If offer card is missing, write to The Reader Service, P.O. Box 1867, Buffalo, NY 14240-1867 or visit www.ReaderService.com

"Oh, no. That's your department."

Meeting their mother face-to-face, if they could locate her, might be so traumatic for Allie and Matt that they'd never recover. But he'd made a promise to them and had to follow through. He heard the sound of footsteps coming down the back hall. "Dad?"

"I'm in here, Matt!"

He came rushing in. "Have you started watching the Utah game yet?"

"Not without you."

Noreen flashed him another smile. "Do you want your spaghetti in here?"

"We'll take care of it. You and Ed do what you want."

"I think we'll run into town and see that *Twilight* film Allie keeps talking about."

"You'll like it," Matt assured her.

Within a few minutes they'd planted themselves in front of the TV and started to watch the recorded game while they ate. By the end of the third quarter it looked like Utah would win if their defense stayed focused. Matt got totally into it, but Colt couldn't concentrate and went back to the kitchen with the empty plates to pour himself a cup of coffee.

While Matt whooped it up because Utah had just scored another touchdown, Colt's cell phone rang. He'd been waiting for the call, needing to hear Kathryn's voice.

It turned out to be her area code, but a different number.

"Hello?"

"Mr. Brenner? This is Jake Halsey."

"I appreciate your phoning me, Mr. Halsey."

"The name's Jake. Kathryn told me about the frightening incident with your daughter. I'm glad she's back home safe with you."

"Your sister-in-law had everything to do with a quick resolution and reunion. I'm indebted to her."

"I'm married to a McFarland. They're the most remarkable people I've ever known. To be honest, I'm still in awe of my wife, Maggie."

Jake had just described Colt's sentiments about Kathryn. Colt liked him for his frank speaking and gripped the phone tighter. "I'm assuming Kathryn explained I'd like to hire you to track down the children's mother, but only if you have the time and inclination."

"I'd do anything for Kathryn."

Jake Halsey appeared to be a remarkable man, too. "Thank you for your willingness to help. The last thing Natalie would want is to be found, but Allie's need to know more about her is so great, she went to Salt Lake without telling me. It's anyone's guess what happens if or when Natalie is located, but my daughter's in crisis."

"I agree," Jake murmured. "Tell you what. Since you're anxious to get going on this, Kathryn and I will make arrangements to take Monday off. Maggie will fly us to Bozeman and we'll brainstorm with you, but only if it's convenient."

As Colt's eyes closed tightly, he could hear Allie coming down the hall. His pulse shouldn't be racing at the thought of Kathryn coming with Jake. "It's an ideal time. Your wife's a pilot?"

"She's a brilliant attorney, too, and has access to resources we'll need." The sisters were superwomen.

"Between the four of us, we'll come up with a game plan."

"Only after we settle on a fee first."

"I wouldn't take your money. Maggie and I want to help."

"What about your son?"

"My stepmother will tend him while we're gone."

When you dealt with the McFarland family, every impediment was removed. "You have no idea how grateful I am. What time do you think you'll fly in? I'll meet your plane."

"Eight-thirty? It'll give us the better part of the day to strategize before we have to head back."

"Perfect." The kids would already have left for school.

"We'll see you on Monday then. If it looks like bad weather will delay our flight, Kathryn will keep you informed. I'm going to ask her to stay on in Bozeman for a few days to do some legwork for me. She has uncanny instincts. Any clue she picks up could be crucial to the case."

He ground his teeth unconsciously. The twins would be ecstatic. As for himself… "I look forward to meeting you, Jake."

"The feeling's mutual, Mr. Brenner."

"Call me Colt. See you Monday morning."

He hung up. Judging by all the noisy excitement coming from his kids in the other room, the Utes had won the game. But it couldn't compare to the conflicted emotions building inside Colt. To see her another time was only asking for trouble, the kind he couldn't afford.

Hell. He already felt like he did the time he'd picked the wrong bull at the Calgary Stampede. The legendary Genghis Kahn had taken him for the ride of his life. The rush had been beyond exhilarating until he found himself hurtling through space. When he woke up in the hospital, he realized a worse concussion would have cost him his life. It had taught him an important lesson.

Some rides you knew in advance to stay away from—like a ride with Kathryn McFarland—because you knew it couldn't last. Another world champion gold buckle was more attainable.

IT WASN'T UNTIL Sunday morning after Kathryn had gotten off the phone with Jake that she remembered Monday was Colt's birthday. She knew his children had to be planning something special for him. Kathryn didn't want to arrive at the ranch empty-handed, yet the wrong gift from her could send out the wrong signal to the elusive rancher.

Since the birth of the twins, he'd been guarding his space jealously against foolish, starry-eyed females. There had to have been an endless line of them over the years, but none had managed to break through the walls of defense he'd set up around his heart.

Maybe she could find something on the internet to do with the rodeo that would suggest a gift idea he wouldn't reject the moment she was out of sight. Ever since he'd told her about the children's mother stealing his gold buckle, she hadn't been able to get it off her mind.

After a half hour of searching, she found a sports memorabilia shop at one of the hotels in Las Vegas. They were auctioning off an officially authenticated, framed poster celebrating thirty-five years of world champion bull riding from the executive's private collection.

Represented were the sketches of four champions in their cowboy hats with their signatures to the side. To her delight she saw a younger Colt's likeness among the grouping, complete with his bold handwriting. It sent her heartbeat skittering off the charts. Beneath the four sketches was an enlarged picture of the gold buckle prize.

This twenty-four-by-thirty-two-inch poster was an absolute treasure.

Rather than go through the online bidding, she made several phone calls until she reached customer service and asked to speak to the manager. After offering him a price he couldn't refuse, he told her the framed poster was hers. She made the transaction with her credit card and told him she'd be in later to claim it.

After she'd clicked off, she called the airport and chartered a plane to Las Vegas. A few hours later, she flew in and picked up her precious purchase. The artist hadn't only caught Colt's chiseled profile, he'd captured his commanding presence and aura of focused energy requisite of a true champion.

While there, she made more enquiries about what other memorabilia she might find on Colt. The manager directed her to a poster shop along the Strip where she found four priceless posters of Colt, all the same picture.

Except for his chaps, he wore black from his Stetson to his boots. He'd been caught in motion on a bull during a championship ride. *Poetry in motion,* in her opinion. It was a spectacular photo.

Kathryn bought all four. One for each twin, one for Noreen and Ed, and one for herself. She would hang it on the library wall next to the bookcase that housed her Louis L'Amour collection.

Almost sick to her stomach with excitement, she flew back to Salt Lake with her secret stash, then drove over to her parents' home to have dinner. While they ate she told them her plans for the next few days. They ended up talking about Whitney's family, who were still waiting to hear something definitive from the police.

Kathryn left their house for the condo feeling guilty that so much pain for the little girl's parents didn't squelch the longing inside her to see Colt again.

After she entered the kitchen, she called Maggie to make final arrangements. Her sister indicated it would be clear weather for flying. They'd be by for her in their car at quarter to six in the morning. "There's no point in telling you to get a good sleep tonight because I know you won't," Maggie teased.

Since Kathryn knew she wouldn't, either, she didn't bother to argue with her sister. Once they said good-night, she pulled a poster from the tube and unfurled it against the fridge door. She used the French bread magnets one of her nieces had given her last Christmas to keep the corners in place.

Just looking at him sent a thrill through her body.

With her eyes glued on him, she phoned Donna so they could set up the schedule of volunteers at the foundation while Kathryn was away. Once that was accomplished, she called her psychiatrist and cancelled Monday's appointment. She would have to phone later to set another date.

While she was at it, she arranged for a rental car to be waiting for them at the Bozeman airport so Colt wouldn't see the presents she was bringing. Finally, she punched in his cell phone number, but this time she had to rein in her emotions to keep them from jumping all over the place.

Don't let him know what the mere thought of him does to you, Kathryn.

Swallowing her disappointment because he didn't pick up, she left a message on his voice mail. "Hi, Colt. I hope all is well with you. I just checked with Maggie. She said it will be good flying weather. One more thing. Jake asked me to let you know he's already arranged a rental car for us, so we should be at the ranch between eighty-thirty and—"

"Kathryn? Don't hang up!" Colt's deep, live voice arced through her, quickening her body.

"You sound out of breath." Would that he was in that condition because of her, but she knew it wasn't the case.

"I was riding in on Lightning when my phone rang, but when I pulled it out of my pocket, it slipped from my hands and fell down a snowy embankment. I had to hunt for it."

The image his words conjured made her smile. He'd made fast work to recover it before she'd clicked off. Colt wasn't a champion bull rider for nothing. "I'm glad it wasn't lost. You might have had to wait until next spring."

He made a low sound in his throat. "My last phone drowned when Matt's lemonade spilled into the cubbyhole of my dashboard."

"Uh-oh." It was her turn to chuckle. "Last summer I was leaning over a castle wall and mine fell into a moat. It's lying somewhere on the bottom, rusting out with all the swords."

A definite laugh rumbled out of him. "Neither of us seems to have had much luck."

Kathryn was having too much fun. *End it now.* "In case yours should short out, I'll make this fast. Maggie said it's good flying weather so we'll be there at eight-thirty, but just to let you know, Jake has arranged for a rental car. He likes to be independent." *Like you.*

"I can relate."

Yup. "We should be to the ranch by nine at the latest."

"Kathryn?"

"Yes?" she answered too breathlessly and could have kicked herself.

"I don't know how to thank you."

"Since Maggie and Jake literally found me, I tell them that all the time. It's a habit I can't break."

"I'm talking about you and what you did for Allie—what you and your family are prepared to do now to help find her mother."

If ever a person was thankful, it was this man, but Kathryn feared she'd never wring anything but gratitude from him.

"This is what we like to do, so enough said. Good night. See you in the morning."

"WHAT'S THIS?" Colt walked in the dining room and discovered Matt already seated at the table. That was a first on a school morning. There were only three places set. "Where are Noreen and Ed?"

"Since she's fixing a special birthday dinner for you tonight, we gave them the morning off to sleep in. I set the table and Allie's fixing your breakfast. We're going to do presents tonight."

On cue his daughter came through the door carrying two plates. "French toast and sausage coming up!" After she put his food in front of him, she gave him a kiss on the cheek. "Happy thirty-sixth, Dad."

A frown marred his features. "Did you have to remind me?" Then Colt grabbed her and gave her a bear hug. She laughed before coming through a second time, bringing her own plate and a mug of coffee for him. They settled down to eat.

Matt's brown eyes studied him. "You look nice, Dad."

"Meaning I usually don't?" he teased.

"Stop fishing for compliments," Allie scolded him. "You've got on a new shirt."

"It's the one your aunt Sherry gave me last Christmas."

"You look like a dude."

"Thanks, Matt. If I'd known I'd get a reaction like this, I'd have worn it before now."

"Black's your best color," his daughter informed him.

"Is that so?" He ate the last piece of toast.

"It makes your eyes look greener. They're really green this morning, like you're excited or something."

Nothing got past Allie. He downed the rest of his coffee. "That's because it's my birthday."

Matt scowled. "You've always said you wished we'd skip yours."

"Did I say that?"

"Yes!" they both answered in unison, exchanging a private glance Colt couldn't help but notice.

"Well, I take it all back. I've loved my surprise breakfast. It was delicious. Thank you both."

"You're welcome," Allie muttered, still staring at him with a puzzled expression.

His son nodded. "There'll be more surprises tonight."

Colt averted his eyes. His children didn't know the half of it. "Much as I hate to break this up, it's time to get you two down to the bus."

"I have to do the dishes first," Matt announced. He jumped up and started clearing the table.

"You stay put, Dad," Allie cautioned before helping her brother.

Together they made short work of it. In a few minutes they joined him in the truck. Colt headed down to the ranch entrance, relieved Kathryn wouldn't be arriving in a snowstorm.

After he pulled to a stop, he got out to give them both an extra hug. "Thanks for breakfast. Love you guys."

"Love you, too. Don't forget. We're coming straight home after school."

Allie nodded. "And don't go out on the range today because we're having your birthday dinner early!"

There was no fear of that. For once something else would be consuming Colt's time right here at home. "I can't wait."

He watched them get on the bus. Since he'd promised

the twins he'd look into finding someone who could try to locate Natalie, he was confident his daughter wouldn't be pulling another disappearance act.

After waving to the bus driver, he checked his watch. Seven-forty-five. Kathryn would be in the air by now. Colt started back. By the time he and Ed had nailed down today's work schedule for the hands, his guests would be arriving. Until then, the idea was to stay busy.

That wasn't a problem in the physical sense. At any given moment, there were tasks needing to be done on the ranch. It was his thoughts that made him restless, the same restlessness he used to get before trying out a new bull shipped up from Mexico.

No matter how prepared he was, some of its moves weren't what he'd anticipated. Kathryn had already knocked the wind out of him several times. The trick was to go the full eight seconds and avoid it administering him the *coup de grâce*.

"WHAT BEAUTIFUL country!" Maggie exclaimed from the front seat of the rental car. Jake had just turned onto the curving road leading up to the ranch. "Look at these walls of pines. They're breathtaking!"

Maggie echoed Kathryn's thoughts, but the feeling of homecoming was so intense she gripped the armrest tighter, unable to say a word.

Jake looked over his shoulder at her. "Are you all right, Kathryn? You're so quiet."

"I'm just remembering the first time I came here. The clouds hung heavy and hid the trees farther up the mountain. With the sun out this morning, you can see everything."

They eventually reached the vale where the ranch became visible. "Incredible," Jake murmured.

"It looks like a Christmas card," Maggie cried softly.

With all of the above, Kathryn concurred. Only this was one card you could drive into and find the ruler of this isolated kingdom at home. Her heart thudded too hard to be natural or healthy.

"Jake? Pull up around the side of the ranch house next to Colt's truck. We'll go in the back door. And one more thing. Leave the trunk popped. I'll take my suitcase in now. Later, when he's not looking, I'll come out to get the presents I brought."

He grinned. "Your wish is my command."

Kathryn let out a guilty sigh. "I'm sorry. I didn't mean to sound bossy."

"Not bossy. Nervous," Maggie said, sending her a secret smile.

Nervous didn't begin to cover what Kathryn was feeling. Every now and then she thought about her life back in Wisconsin and shuddered to think that if Maggie and Jake hadn't found her, she would never have met Colton Brenner. She scrambled out the backseat of the car and hurried to retrieve her bag from the trunk.

It was a good thing she'd moved fast because Colt had come out of the house, a tall dark figure in a black shirt and jeans bearing down on them with those powerful legs. Just in time she'd lowered the trunk lid so it looked closed, but wasn't.

"Welcome to the Circle B." He shook Jake's and

Maggie's hands before wresting Kathryn's suitcase from her. Their eyes met. The green of his irises matched the color of the pines.

"Hello, Colt," Somehow she'd managed to keep her voice from shaking. At the first sight of him, it was always an event that rearranged the atoms in her body. "It's nice to be back." Heavens, he looked so wonderful, she was in danger of falling straight into him.

"The children won't believe it when they get home from school and find you here."

"They didn't know we were coming?"

He smiled, making him irresistible. "If I'd told them, there would have been a war to get them to go to school and I would have lost."

She laughed. "I'm looking forward to seeing them, too."

"Let's get you inside so you can freshen up." Colt led them through the back entrance, where they removed their parkas. He turned to Jake. "If you want to use the guest bathroom down here, the women are welcome to go up to Kathryn's room."

He carried her suitcase upstairs and put it inside the guest-room door. His gaze locked with Kathryn's. "When you come down, Jake and I will be in the family room."

"We'll be there in a minute."

As soon as he left and shut the door, Maggie's brows lifted. "*Kathryn's* room? Sounds like you're already part of the family."

"Don't be ridiculous!"

"I'm only stating the obvious," she said before closing the bathroom door.

Taking advantage of the time, Kathryn zipped over to Allie's room and used her bathroom before rejoining her sister. "You've got the wrong idea about Colt," she said without preamble. "He's not interested in me personally. The complicated man has led an *un*complicated life for years and that's not going to change."

Maggie put her hands on Kathryn's shoulders. "Listen to me, little sister. It already has changed or he wouldn't have come to Salt Lake to see you. He has money. He could hire an army of people to look for his ex-wife. Why didn't he?"

"Because Allie asked *me* for help. And because a miracle happened to our family and she believes I'll be able to perform one for hers. I can tell you right now that after what Allie pulled, Colt's vulnerability over his children is so great, he'd do anything for them."

"That goes without saying, but why are you fighting me on this?"

"I'm not!"

"Yes, you are. What aren't you telling me?"

For once Maggie had made her cross. "He's grateful to me."

"Of course he is."

"But that's all!"

Maggie let go of her. "You're afraid of something. Tell me what it is."

She lowered her head. "I don't know exactly."

"I think you do."

"All right, then." She lifted her chin. "If you must know, I don't want to be like Steve."

Her sister blinked. "What do you mean?"

"He hung around you for years hoping for any crumbs

you would throw his way. But you never noticed him or any man until Jake came along and rocked your world." She swallowed hard. "I'm not like Steve. I'd rather die first," she whispered.

"Your situation is entirely different from mine. As for Colt Brenner, he's thrown you more than a crumb," her sister insisted.

"Wrong. Let me ask you a question. Who suggested I stay on a few days to do some of Jake's legwork here? Colt or Jake?"

"Jake."

"Don't you see? He didn't leave Colt a choice."

"I have a feeling he's secretly pleased the way things are turning out."

"No. He's been single sixteen years for a reason."

Maggie's expression sobered. "If you really believe that, then check into a motel in Bozeman after you drop us off at the airport and get busy running down evidence for Jake. You know I'll do my part. Once the objective has been accomplished and Colt doesn't need your services any longer, walk away from him and see what happens."

Nothing will happen. But no one gave sounder advice than Maggie. *Get the job done you've been asked you to do, then get out!*

On a gush of love for her sister, Kathryn hugged her hard. "You're brilliant! I'm ready to go downstairs and dig in."

"Good." With their arms around each other, they left the bedroom.

Kathryn knew the way to the family room, but the second she entered it, her heart rate went into hyperdrive at the sight of the two attractive males talking in deep concentration in front of the fire.

She felt a fresh stab of pain because she could sense Colt was anxious to catch up to his ex-wife. Natalie Brenner had to have been unforgettable for him to have married her within two weeks of meeting her and then go all these years without marrying again.

Chapter Seven

At noon, Jake closed the notebook he'd brought to keep a record. His steel-blue gaze shot to Colt's. "We've accomplished as much as we can for the moment."

Colt glanced at his watch. Two and a half hours of discussing strategies with these remarkable people had flown by. Once during their session around the dining-room table, Kathryn had excused herself for a few minutes. Except for Noreen who'd supplied food and coffee, they'd worked undisturbed.

"To tell you how grateful I am for your time and help wouldn't begin to cover how I feel."

Maggie smiled. Both women were so gorgeous, Colt could only marvel. "We'll all hope it doesn't take as long as it did to find my baby sister."

Kathryn got up from the table. "Twenty-six years will put Allie and Matt at forty-one." She'd done the math. "We can do better, right? I'll drop you at the airport so I can have a car." She looked at her family without including Colt.

If it was intentional, he didn't like it. "My Xterra's at your disposal while you're here, Kathryn."

She glanced at him. "I appreciate that, but I understand Noreen uses it to shop and pick up the kids from the school bus. Your routine shouldn't be interrupted because of me. I'll be scouting around talking to people on my own timetable."

"That's settled, then," Jake broke in. "I understand Noreen is over at her house. Please tell her how much we enjoyed the food."

"I'll be happy to."

"Shall we go, darling?" Jake rose to his feet to help his wife.

Colt followed the three of them through the house to the back entrance, where Kathryn put on her parka too fast for him to be of use. He decided it was a habit she'd developed over all the years she'd been forced to look out for herself.

"You live in paradise and have an absolutely beautiful home!" Maggie exclaimed on the way to the car. "This valley opens up like a stairway to heaven."

"Kathryn thinks it should be called the Cloud Bottom Ranch."

Laughter rippled out of Maggie. "That sounds like something my imaginative sister would say."

He stole a covert glance at Kathryn, whose cheeks looked flushed, before she climbed in the backseat behind Maggie. Jake shook his hand one more time before getting in the driver's seat.

Colt moved closer and tapped on Kathryn's window so she'd open it. He stared down into eyes as blue as Montana's big sky country. "The kids will be home by three-thirty. It'll make their day to find you here."

"I'll be back in time."

Not by a flicker of an eyelash or an inflection in her

voice could he detect what was going on inside her. To his irritation, she closed the window, putting a barrier between them when he wasn't ready for it. But as he turned away, he noticed the rapid throbbing of the pulse at her throat. It couldn't be the altitude doing all that to her.

He waved off his guests before heading back inside the house, but once at his desk in the den he couldn't concentrate on the accounts. After an hour, he gave up.

Damn if it wasn't happening to him…

That deep ache only the right woman could arouse, with her alluring scent and mysterious smile. How could he not crave the accidental brush of her hip against his or her sudden slight intake of breath in an unguarded moment?

Colt couldn't begin to count the ways the voluptuous shape of her mouth entranced him—or the way the unexpected compassion in those blue depths for someone else's stolen child could move him to tears.

When the phone rang, he clicked on without checking the caller ID and almost said her name. "Hello?"

"How does it feel to be another year older?"

"Sherry?"

She laughed. "Who else? You sound odd."

"I'm afraid my mind was on something else." *Someone else.*

"I thought I'd better get in a phone call before you start celebrating. Did our presents reach you in time?"

"They came two days ago, but after the great Thanksgiving you gave us, you shouldn't have sent anything."

"Colt! You're impossible!"

"Sorry. I didn't mean to sound ungrateful."

"I know," she murmured. "I wish we could be there to celebrate with you, but Bob couldn't get away. This is his busy time doing audits."

"But you'll be coming to our place for Christmas, right?" Except that he couldn't think that far ahead. He was still working on the countdown until Kathryn returned from town.

"You couldn't keep us away. Now tell me what's being planned for your birthday?"

"I'm not sure. The kids have been cooking up something with Noreen." *As for* my *surprise…*

"Then it's bound to be special because they love you to death. So do I."

"The feeling's mutual, Sherry. Thanks for making my day. I'll phone you tomorrow and give you the details."

"You'd better!"

After they rang off, he realized he couldn't stay in the house any longer without climbing walls knowing Kathryn wasn't far away. Why not surprise the kids and be there waiting for them when school was out? Pushing himself away from his desk, he strode through the house for his hat and jacket.

Once in the car, he phoned Noreen and told her to be on the watch for Kathryn. He was going to pick up the twins.

THE SILVER SPUR MOTEL on the outskirts of Bozeman provided exactly what Kathryn wanted. After seeing Maggie and Jake off at the airport, she registered at the front desk before driving around to Number Ten. The tiny room, with its log cabin walls, felt warm and she could park in front of it. No fuss, no bother.

While she'd been with her family and Colt earlier, she'd excused herself long enough to put her suitcase back in the trunk and bring in the presents for him. Once his birthday party was over, she'd tell the twins she had business in town and leave.

He'd hired Jake to track down Natalie. Though Kathryn would be helping her brother-in-law, she refused to use it as an excuse to stay at the ranch house. Colt didn't want her there, so the less interaction she had with his children the better. This was the best plan.

Before she drove back to the ranch, she took off her navy two-piece wool suit and changed into jeans and a café au lait long-sleeved blouse with a cream-colored crocheted vest. She'd already styled her hair in a French braid that morning and decided to leave the gold studs in her ears.

In deference to her cowboy mood, Kathryn pulled on the brown leather boots she always wore riding with her family. She liked the idea of being taller. It would put her at less of a disadvantage around Colt.

A fresh coat of coral frost lipstick, a little peach-scented lotion and she was ready to go.

With every mile that brought her closer to the ranch, she could feel more heat radiating from her body. By the time she'd parked the rental car at the side of the house, she was a trembling mass of emotions. The fact that the Xterra was missing only heightened her sense of anticipation.

Noreen greeted her at the back door. "I saw you

coming. Colt's gone for the twins. Come in and make yourself comfortable."

Kathryn followed her through the house to the dining room. "Something smells delicious."

"Matt asked me to make barbecued spareribs. It's one of Colt's favorite meals."

"It's one of mine, too. How can I help you?"

"Everything's ready except the decorations. Allie had visions of blue and white streamers hanging crisscross fashion above the table. Ed was going to do it, but he's been delayed. I brought in the ladder."

"I'm taller. Put me to work."

"That would be wonderful."

Kathryn eyed things critically. "Let's fasten them from the chandelier to the window frames. I'll twist them first."

Before long they'd transformed the room. She climbed back down. "There!"

Noreen beamed. "It's perfect."

"I think so, too. Where does the ladder go?"

"On a couple of hooks in the storeroom behind the kitchen. If you're going to do that, I'll run back to the other house and get changed."

"Go ahead."

Grabbing the leftover streamers and tape, Kathryn carried everything through the kitchen to a doorway at the other end. She turned on the light and found an empty space for the crepe paper on one of the shelves. There were hooks on the opposite wall. As she started for them, she heard Colt's voice coming from the kitchen. "Noreen?"

"She's at her house!"

The next thing Kathryn knew, he'd moved behind her and put the ladder in place. Her mouth went dry because she was trapped between his arms with her back against his chest. The strong pounding of his heart had already reset the rhythm of hers. Heat enveloped her body.

"Colt, you can let me go now."

"I could, but I don't want to," he whispered against the side of her neck. His hands slid around her waist, bringing her closer so there was no air between them. "It isn't often I find such a tempting morsel in my store-room. Surely you wouldn't deny me this simple pleasure on my birthday."

She sucked in her breath. "The twins will see us."

His warm breath at her nape sent sensation after exquisite sensation through her nervous system. "They dashed upstairs to do the last of their clandestine plotting."

"D-do they know I'm here?" she stammered helplessly.

"They saw the car, but assumed it was someone on ranch business waiting for me. Allie begged me to get rid of them fast."

"You should take her advice."

"Not until I've been given my birthday kiss."

"That wouldn't be a good idea." Her voice shook.

"I disagree." He turned her around so fast her head swam. While she was still reeling, he cupped her hot cheeks with his hands and lowered his mouth to hers.

Kathryn had wanted this for so long she melted against him, but his tender kiss was over before he'd allowed her to kiss him back. She moaned as he relinquished her lips. "That's for being an angel to my little girl. I'll never forget."

Gratitude. Colt had just bestowed the kiss of death.

They both heard excited voices that were growing louder. His hands slowly fell away from her face. "I guess it's time to reveal the mystery guest."

Struggling to recover from the pain, Kathryn rushed into the kitchen at the same time the twins made an appearance.

"Katy!" She saw them staring at her and Colt as if they couldn't believe their eyes.

"Your father hired my brother-in-law to track down your mother. Jake asked me to do some research for him in Bozeman, so I'm here for a day or two."

"Yes!" Allie squealed.

Realizing they needed more of an explanation, she said, "Since Ed was late, I volunteered to string up the decorations."

"I helped Kathryn put the ladder away," their father added in a wry tone.

At that remark, she might have blushed if Colt had kissed her with passion, but he wasn't capable of that emotion, at least not with her. The only way to handle this was to be a friend to him and his children.

"Thank goodness your dad arrived in time to prevent it from falling on my head!"

Matt let out a bark of laughter. Allie said, "The dining room looks awesome."

Kathryn smiled. "I can't take any credit. Noreen said the streamers were your idea."

"But you made everything beautiful. Will you come upstairs with me for a minute?"

"Sure. Excuse us," she called out to Colt without looking at him.

"Don't be long, ladies. It's my birthday and I'm ready to party."

Allie laughed. "I thought you were upset at being a year older! Come on, Katy."

Together they hurried through the house and up the stairs to Allie's bedroom. Kathryn eyed Colt's flushed-faced daughter. "You look fully recovered from your flu."

"I feel great!"

"That makes me very happy."

Her brown eyes glowed. "Your being here for Dad's party is perfect!"

"Jake took the day off from his work so my sister could fly us here this morning for a talk with your father. When I realized we would be arriving on his birthday, I brought a present that I thought you and Matt could give him along with your other gifts. It's guaranteed to be a hit. I'll get it."

Allie picked up a shopping bag full of presents and followed her to the guest bedroom.

"Here. Take this one in your other hand." Kathryn handed her the framed, gift-wrapped poster. "I'll bring my other presents." After putting the rolled-up posters beneath her arms, she said, "Let's go before your father gets too impatient."

They started down the stairs. "He's going to have a cow when he sees all this!"

Kathryn tried to keep a straight face. "Is that good or bad?"

"Definitely good," Colt answered for his daughter.

There was nothing wrong with his hearing. He stood in the foyer with Matt. His eyes locked with Kathryn's. She couldn't read what was behind that enigmatic gaze. If he feared she was hoping for a repeat performance of what had happened in the storeroom, he didn't need to worry. His grateful tribute had cured her.

Matt rocked on his cowboy boots. "Noreen's got everything ready."

They proceeded to the dining room. It was growing darker out. The addition of a lovely cloth, candlelight and a decorated chocolate cake forming the centerpiece provided the magical touches to the birthday feast. Kathryn read, "Happy 36, Dad."

"Here. Let me." Ed, the older, dark blond rancher now free of his cast, helped Allie spread her packages around the pile already visible on the hunt board. Both he and Colt gave Allie a curious stare as he lifted the framed poster and rested it against the wall.

While Matt helped Kathryn to the table, Colt helped his daughter. Noreen brought the ribs from the kitchen. Ed said grace and they were ready to eat.

For the next half hour, conversation centered around the twins and their latest activities. Kathryn mostly listened, only now and then asking a question. Throughout the delicious meal she avoided looking at Colt.

Once they'd sung "Happy Birthday" and had eaten cake, Matt and Allie took turns giving their dad a present to open. Every gift appeared to be a winner: a robe, sweats, cologne, socks, a Western shirt, leather gloves, ski gloves, new ski goggles, a couple of T-shirts...everything for the well-dressed rancher.

Kathryn finally dared to smile at Colt. "That's quite

a haul. I think it's time somebody else around here got a present." Five pairs of eyes blinked in surprise. "Matt? Will you hand one of those cylinders to Noreen and Ed? Then give one to Allie and take one for yourself."

While everyone started unwrapping their gifts, Colt stared at Kathryn with a bemused expression on his rugged face.

The responses were everything she could have hoped for. Cries of "Dad! Colt!" resounded as they unraveled the posters of the beloved man seated at the head of the table. "Oh, my gosh! You look so young!"

Allie ran over to Kathryn. "Where did you get this?" she cried out with tears in her eyes. "I *love* it! I can't wait to show all my friends! They're going to die!"

"You're so awesome, Dad!" Matt's voice croaked. "Rich has got to see this!" He stood in the corner of the room examining it.

Noreen and Ed's eyes grew misty as they handed their poster of the legendary rodeo champion to Colt for him to see. Ed handed him a pen. "I want your autograph. This could be worth a fortune someday."

Kathryn understood everyone's joy because she felt it herself, but it was time to make her exit. Otherwise she might never be able to pry herself away.

"Happy birthday, Colt." She got up from the table. "Thanks to all of you for letting me be part of this celebration. Noreen? The food was out of this world, but now I'm afraid I have to leave."

Allie looked stricken. "Where are you going?"

"Back to my motel in Bozeman."

"Motel?" the twins moaned together.

"Yes. While you people have a whole night of

celebrating ahead of you, I need to accomplish a day's worth of foundation work plus some business for Jake before tomorrow morning."

"But you *can't* go yet!"

"Kathryn said she had to leave," Colt reminded his daughter in a voice of understated authority. "She flew here from Salt Lake to help us find your mother, remember? Let's let her get on with her jobs. Matt? Would you bring down her suitcase, please?"

"Sure."

"Don't bother to go up, Matt. I left it at the motel." Avoiding Colt's piercing gaze, she looked at Allie. "I think there's one more gift your father hasn't opened yet. Right?"

"Yes," the girl whispered.

"Then have fun. I'll see myself out."

Kathryn hurried through the house to the back room, where she grabbed her purse and parka. Within a minute, she'd reached the car and was headed for town.

Colt didn't want her getting any more attached to his children and was glad she'd done the right thing by leaving. That was why he hadn't tried to stop her. Any goodbye had been said in the storeroom behind the kitchen.

Her pain went too deep for tears. Frozen-faced, she drove straight to her motel needing to talk to Maggie.

Maybe her sister had radar because the second she closed the door to the room, her cell phone rang. She pulled it from her purse and checked the caller ID. It was Donna.

Her stomach knotted because her assistant wouldn't call this late at night unless she had important news.

"Hello?"

"Kathryn?"

Just the way Donna said her name, she knew what she was about to say. "That body was Whitney's, wasn't it?"

"Yes."

Hot tears spurted from her eyes. "I have to get off the phone now and call my parents. Thank you for letting me know."

"Of course."

But the second Kathryn hung up, she threw herself across the bed and sobbed because a miracle hadn't happened for that little girl's family. She sobbed for all the helpless kidnapped children who this very night were being molested or killed somewhere in the world. Not even everything the McFarland Foundation could do had prevented this crime against Whitney.

Beyond heartsick, she lay there for a long time in such a deep sorrow, she didn't realize her phone was ringing. Finally stirring, she sat up and looked at the caller ID. It was her sister. She clicked on.

"Maggie?"

"I've been on the phone with the folks. Did you hear about Whitney?"

"Yes. I just got off the phone with Donna."

Neither of them spoke for a minute. There were no platitudes they could say to comfort each other. Another tragedy had befallen another child. Yet next to her grief lay her guilt for thinking of Colt right now and how incomprehensible it would have been if Allie had been lost to him forever.

"How was the birthday party?" her sister ventured. "You know what I mean."

"The surprise was everything I could have hoped for. Allie and Matt loved the posters, but I left before Colt opened the framed one."

"Why did you do that?"

"Because I got an answer earlier tonight."

"Translation please."

Knowing Maggie wouldn't let it go, Kathryn launched into an explanation of what had happened in the storeroom. "I was ready to explode like a volcano, but his brief, chaste thank-you kiss cooled everything down. He might as well have been the Pope giving me a benediction for my goodness."

Instead of her sister coming right back with the assurance that Kathryn had misread the situation, she said something entirely different. "You were right about him being a complicated man."

Maggie's quiet response set off an alarm bell. There was a message behind her words, otherwise she would have waited until Kathryn had returned to Salt Lake to talk about the little girl who'd been murdered. Kathryn gripped her phone tighter. "What do you know that I don't?"

"While you and I were upstairs at his ranch house this morning, Colt confided something to Jake. Maybe you already know what it is and have chosen not to tell me."

"Tell you what?" Her voice shook.

"He never divorced his wife."

"See, Dad? This looks perfect in here! Everyone who comes in will notice it before anything else!"

With Colt's children helping Ed and Noreen, a little rearranging had gone on and now the framed poster with protective glass hung on one of the walls in the family room. They'd wanted to put it in his den, but he'd ruled it out. Colt used that room to conduct business with the public and disliked the idea of his awards being on display. At least the family room was a little more private.

After Natalie had taken off years earlier, any of the stuff from his rodeo days he'd thrown in a box in the storage shed behind the old house. It was now covered with other boxes. Neither the twins nor the Walters had any idea of its existence. That was the way he'd wanted it. But he couldn't get away with doing the same thing to Kathryn's gift. His children wouldn't hear of it.

She'd transformed his birthday party into something else. The posters dredged up memories he'd suppressed for so long, he'd almost forgotten what those sweet days were like when he was single and hungry for a bull-riding title that would help make his fortune.

No one but Kathryn McFarland could have located that framed poster, let alone managed to get the collector to part with it. No doubt she'd been robbed of her money and had enriched the man's coffers by several thousand dollars, but money in and of itself meant nothing to her.

She'd go to any lengths without counting the cost in order to bring happiness to someone else. Except for disappearing to a motel this evening, she'd made Colt's twins ecstatic.

Though she was a flesh-and-blood woman whose mouth he could still taste on his lips, he didn't doubt he'd kissed an angel earlier. As anyone knew, angels went about doing good, especially this angel whose joy at being found after her long captivity might have turned her into another kind of captive. One who couldn't do enough for others. *One you might never be able to pin down, Brenner.*

That was Colt's new agony.

When he'd heard the children coming into the kitchen before dinner, it had almost killed him to let go of Kathryn, but what choice did he have when he was so on fire for her that he still trembled at the thought of holding her again?

"Dad? I thought you wanted to play Boggle."

His son's voice jerked him back to the present. "I do."

"Then let's get started."

Colt joined his children at the card table in front of the fire. A half hour later Allie said, "I win again! We need to play this on your birthday more often."

"Yeah," Matt chimed in. "You haven't won once. Usually you beat us by at least fifteen extra words."

"That's because you guys gave me such a great party I can't concentrate. Now it's time for bed." The twins protested, but he reminded them they had school in the morning.

Allie lingered on the stairs, holding her poster. "Do you think Katy will come over tomorrow?" It was the first time her name had been mentioned in the past hour.

He shook his head. "My guess is she'll do her work and fly back to Salt Lake. She's on a busy schedule trying to help you, honey."

Her downfallen expression didn't escape him. "I know. Well, good night."

Colt hugged her. "Thanks for a wonderful birthday."

Matt came loping into the foyer with his poster. "Hey, Dad. I just got off the phone with Rich. Would you be willing to train us how to ride a bull?"

Somehow Colt had known that question was coming. Kathryn had opened up the proverbial Pandora's box. "Why don't we talk about it tomorrow?"

His son grinned. "I'm holding you to it. 'Night." They high-fived each other before he bounded up the stairs after Allie.

The second he saw his son's boots disappear, Colt wheeled around and left the house, grabbing his hat and jacket on the way. Once in the truck, he phoned Noreen, letting her know he had an errand to run and would be back on the ranch in a couple of hours. There'd be no sleep for him until he'd dropped in on Kathryn and thanked her for her gifts in person.

At the third motel he spotted her rental car in front of Number Ten. Though the curtains were drawn, he could tell her light was on. He levered himself from the cab. A few steps to the door and he rapped on it. If he'd phoned her first, she would have put him off. This way she had to do it in person.

"Kathryn? It's Colt."

She didn't keep him waiting long, but when she opened the door fully dressed, she was on the phone and motioned for him to come in. Though he couldn't see tears, he knew she'd been crying and had a gut notion why. As he closed the door, he heard her say good-night to her mother before hanging up.

"Was it Whitney's body?" he whispered.

Her beautiful face crumpled in pain. She had no words. All he could do was pull her into his arms and try to comfort her, but he'd never felt so helpless in his life.

"Oh, Colt! This world can be so terrible, yet so wonderful, too."

He kissed the side of her temple. "It was wonderful tonight. I opened my last present and discovered that something I'd treasured and thought lost forever had been returned."

"I'm glad it made you happy."

"The children have hung it in the family room. That's twice Kathryn McFarland has restored something priceless to me."

She eased out of his arms. With a small smile she said, "I hear good things come in threes. Here's hoping we find your wife before long."

Colt heard her distinctly. She'd said *wife*—not ex, not Natalie, not the children's mother.

"So Jake has already told you."

"After they flew home, he started in on the investigation and mentioned it to Maggie. She didn't know if I knew or not, but it doesn't matter."

"What? That I'm still married?"

"That's your own business."

Chapter Eight

Her phone had started ringing. "Excuse me, Colt. I need to see who this is." She picked up. "Hi, Kit. It's good to hear your voice, but I've got someone with me. I'll call you back in a few minutes."

Kathryn gave him an inscrutable blue stare and the tension between them caused him to bite down hard. "What I have on my mind is going to take some time. If you'd like, I'll wait in the truck until you're through talking to your sister-in-law, even if it means I have to sit out there half the night." He wanted to let her know he meant business.

He was counting on her good manners not to tell him to get the hell out of her motel room *now*.

The fight going on inside her went on for a full minute before she said, "I'll phone Kit and tell her I'll talk to her tomorrow. She's as upset about Whitney as the rest of us."

Colt expelled the air from his lungs. While she called her sister-in-law back, he removed his hat and jacket and sat down on one of the two chairs propped near the table.

He liked it that the motel room was claustrophobic.

Kathryn only had two places to sit—the bed that took up most of the room or the other chair.

She chose the safer course, but it brought her close enough that their boots brushed. Much as he wanted to pull her onto his lap and kiss them both into oblivion, he turned in order to extend his long legs away from her. "I need to explain."

She shook her beautiful blond head. "It's not necessary."

Colt couldn't have felt more gutted if he'd been stomped unconscious by a bull. "It is to *me*," he fired back. "Jake needed to know about my marital status up front, but I preferred not to discuss it in front of you and your sister. Call it cowardice if you want. When he talked to me on the phone the other day, he told me he'd do anything for you, so I should have guessed he would start his investigation the minute he got back to Salt Lake. It's how you McFarlands operate."

Kathryn looked away.

"Whether you believe me or not, I came here tonight to talk to you about it in private. Until now, the time never seemed right."

"You don't have to tell me."

"You deserve the whole truth." He sat forward. "In the beginning, I was too involved in taking care of my premature babies and running the ranch to think about anything else. I figured that one day I'd hear from her through an attorney that she wanted a divorce. That suited me fine. I was in no hurry to rush into another ill-fated marriage."

Her pained eyes searched his. "No one would be."

"When she did make contact, I planned to get my

buckle back. The fact that I never heard from her again proved how much she didn't want to get caught."

"I don't know how you lived through that experience."

"The twins became my whole world."

She smiled. "Naturally. They're wonderful."

"After my grandparents died, I let go of my anger and made up my mind to be the best father I could. The ranch began to prosper and I found joy in my children. There were women, yet attractive as they were, I couldn't picture any of them being the kind of mother my twins needed."

"You'd lost a lot of trust," Kathryn murmured.

He nodded. "One or two of those women wanted to get married. I probably should have had Natalie declared legally dead so that could happen, but the desire wasn't strong enough to go to the trouble." He rubbed the back of his neck. "If Jake can't find her, then I'll go that route."

"Are the twins aware you're still married to their mother?"

Colt studied her through shuttered lids. "No. But if they raise that question, I'll tell them." After a pause, "Will you forgive me?"

She stirred in the chair. "There's nothing to forgive."

"Prove it and we'll go over to the Westerner for a drink and a dance. They have a good live band. It'll top off my birthday."

"That's right. It's your birthday." She glanced at her watch. "For another hour, anyway."

"Come on."

He stood up and reached for her parka in the closet. This time, she had to let him help her. The need to touch her had become paramount to his existence. She handed him his hat and they went out the door into the cold night.

Their arms and hips brushed as he opened the truck door for her, electrifying his body. It was a good thing the Westerner was only two miles away. The desire to have her in his arms was consuming him.

Colt hadn't been inside the bar for several years. The place was swinging. They'd heard the country music out in the parking lot.

"Hey, Colt!" several of his younger hands called out to him. He nodded to them. Every man's eyes had locked on to Kathryn while he ushered her through the crowd. With a packed dance floor, it was slow maneuvering. The wolf whistles and comments kept coming.

He whispered near her ear, "No one's seen anyone like you in here before. Stick close to me." His hands stayed on her shoulders from behind until he'd guided her to a free booth in the corner. He removed their parkas before sitting next to her.

A cheeky waitress came over to take their order. "Coffee for me," Kathryn said.

"Make that two coffees, one with cream and sugar." After the waitress left, the guy at the mike called for a round of line dancing. Colt eyed the gorgeous woman squeezed in the booth next to him. "Let's do it."

He grasped her hand and took her out on the floor to the end of the last row. For the next little while, he had the time of his life going through the motions with the best dancer in the room. Every male in the place envied him. *Eat your hearts out.*

Eventually they returned to the booth to drink their coffee. "Where did you learn to move like that?"

"Cord taught me and Kit. He's a cowboy at heart and would rather line dance than just about anything, but I think you could teach him a few steps."

"I got a lot of practice during my rodeo days. After an event, a bunch of us would head for the nearest bar to unwind."

"When did you start bull riding?"

"At Matt's age."

"Has he tried it yet?"

"My son's been making noises to learn, but after you showered your gifts on us tonight, he and his friend Rich have it all planned that I'm going to teach them the fundamentals starting this coming weekend."

She looked alarmed. "Does that bother you?"

"No. It's a great sport. If he wants to try to get good at it, there's nothing more challenging or exciting except maybe a slow dance with you." Color spilled into her cheeks. "Before this place closes, how about it?"

Dancing gave him a legitimate excuse to cling to her voluptuous body. They fit together as if they'd been made for each other. Way too soon, the band played their last song, bringing an end to the enchantment.

Colt protested inwardly as he helped Kathryn back into the truck. He'd wanted to keep her in his arms all night. Out on that floor he'd forgotten he was still legally married. For a while, nothing mattered but the physical and mental closeness they shared.

"Did you just say something?" he asked as they headed for the motel.

"Yes. I was thinking about your gold buckle. I have a hunch it could be the key to putting us on Natalie's trail. What exact time frame are we talking about from the moment you won the world championship until she left?"

They were back to the investigation. "The twins were premature and born in July. She left in August. Approximately eight and a half months."

"Did you go straight to Montana after you'd won?"

"We stayed in Las Vegas for another two days, then drove to the ranch in my old pickup truck."

"So before you even left Las Vegas, she could have gone behind your back and talked to a contact about selling your gold buckle to some collector for a big price?"

"It's possible. Knowing what I know now, Natalie was capable of anything." He didn't want to talk about her.

"Did you still have it when you reached the ranch?"

How could Kathryn be talking like this after what they'd been doing for the past hour? "It doesn't work that way. I was presented my award, but they sent it back to Montana Silversmiths to have my name hand-lettered in gold on it. I received it by overnight courier a month later."

"Did it come with a special belt?"

"There's no belt. My grandparents kept it in a place of honor on the mantel along with my other awards. My grandmother was the first to notice it was missing.

Natalie must have taken it the day she left the house for good."

By now they'd reached the Silver Spur and she'd already opened the truck door. Colt climbed out to help her down, but he didn't know how he was going to leave her. For sixteen years he'd existed without her. Now she'd started a fire in him that would never go out. Every second with her made it burn hotter.

When she opened the motel-room door, he went inside with her, ostensibly to make sure she was safe. He checked the bathroom and the closet. "I wish you'd come back to the ranch with me tonight. I'd feel better."

"Thank you for caring, but I'll be fine."

He'd been studying her appealing features all night and couldn't get enough of them. "What's your agenda tomorrow?"

"A dozen different things. I plan to get an early start."

"I'll take you to dinner."

"That would be lovely, but I might not be here."

"Why?" he demanded.

"If I've accomplished everything Jake wants, I'll fly home in the afternoon."

"With Maggie?"

She nodded.

His hands balled into fists. "Don't you ever stop to enjoy yourself?"

She flashed him a breezy smile. "I've been doing that all day. Thank you for a wonderful night of dancing. For thirty-six years, you're remarkably good. It must be the bull rider in you. Good night, Colt. I'll be in touch."

KATHRYN ENTERED her psychiatrist's empty reception room at nine and waited until he appeared at the door of his private office, telling her to come in. She sat down opposite his desk. He was a short, balding man who wore steel-rimmed glasses.

"I'm sorry I couldn't come in last week. I've had to go out of town several times on child advocacy business."

He smiled. "These appointments are for you, not me."

"I realize that." She'd been coming to Dr. Morrow's office for over four years. He was a friend who knew her inside and out, but one of these days he would retire. She couldn't imagine not having him in her life. Lately it seemed her problems were getting worse, not better. What would she do without him? The thought sent her into a panic.

"I happened to see you on last night's news."

She nodded. "Our family attended Whitney's funeral yesterday morning. I think half the city must have been there." The intrusion of the TV networks had been too much.

Her doctor sat with his elbows on the desk, tapping his fingertips together. "Why did you go?"

His question stunned her. "You mean our family?"

"No. *You.*"

Kathryn frowned. "Because I run the foundation."

"Besides that. I want you to think very hard. Before our session ends, I'd like an answer." He sat back in the chair. "What are you doing for fun these days?"

"Fun?"

Her brother had asked her the same question the other day.

"You don't have any," he commented. "When you first came to me and described Anna Buric's life in Wisconsin, this is what you said." He opened a folder on his desk. "I'm going to read from my notes.

"Some days were good when Nelly brought me books to read. We had fun cooking in the bakery. Sometimes she would take me driving around the farm. Those were good times. On my days off I climbed trees in the apple orchard with the younger children. I liked reading stories to the littlest ones. It was like I was their mother. I used to pretend they were my children. That was fun."

Kathryn averted her eyes.

"Isn't it interesting that my notes on Kathryn McFarland—once all the joy of reunion had finally died down—don't mention anything about having fun."

"That's not true!" she protested. She'd had so much fun with Colt on his birthday that she'd come close to begging him to stay the night with her.

"I'm afraid it is. Your life is all about work. Why?"

"Because it's what my family does."

"You mean to tell me your brothers and sister don't ever have any fun?"

"No. Of course not. They do all kinds of fun things. They ski and ride horses. They recently went to the Utah football game together."

"Did you go to the last one?"

"No."

"Why not?"

"I had foundation business."

"Let me ask you another question. You were planning

to move out of the McFarland Tower and get your own house. Have you done that yet?"

"No."

"Why?"

"Because there's no place more convenient to my work."

"Have you joined that book club your friend suggested?"

"No. I never have the time."

"What about a pet? We talked about that before, too."

"Much as I'd like one, with my schedule I decided I wouldn't be able to give it the love and attention it deserves."

He took off his glasses and rubbed his eyes. "Have you done any dating since you turned down Steve's proposal?"

"No."

"I see. Have you formulated an answer to my initial question?"

In a rare show of temper she said, "Is this really necessary? You know very well I want to give back what my parents sacrificed for me during all those years I was missing."

"That's a lofty goal, but one that's quite impossible. You're not your parents. It isn't the same situation."

"I know that."

"No, I don't think you do. They carved out a life for themselves. Now it's up to you to live the one destiny intended for you, not the one you assume you have to live in order to make up for all their pain."

There'd been occasions when Dr. Morrow had made

her angry, but never more so than now. She felt the blood heat her cheeks.

"Guilt has a lot to answer for in this world, Kathryn. You feel more guilt than most people because of the new life you don't think you deserve since you were found. That's why it rips you apart whenever another child is kidnapped and killed."

Her eyes stung with salty tears.

"Guilt is driving you to be all things to all people. Unfortunately if you're not careful, it's going to break you."

Colt had said virtually the same thing when she'd accompanied Allie home from Salt Lake.

"You're a healthy, lovely woman who, since your kidnapping, has taken on the senseless obligation of owing your parents your life. I don't believe for a second that's what they want. This crusade to be like them and live up to the model they established through the Kathryn McFarland Foundation has overtaken your life."

She lowered her head. "You make me sound like a freak."

"That's one description for a hopeless workaholic. You spent the first twenty-six years wishing you could find your parents. Once you did, you've spent the past four years trying to make it up to them. It's past time you thought outside the box and did something that has nothing to do with the past thirty years. Otherwise, you'll remain single and burn out early. Is that what you really want?"

"No."

"*No?* That's the first time you've ever admitted it to me. What's happened since our last session?"

She squirmed. "I'd rather not talk about it."

"If not to me, then who?"

"It's not that, Dr. Morrow."

"You've met a man."

Heat crept through her body. "Colt's married with teenage children and owns a cattle ranch in Montana."

"At least he's flesh and blood, not your fantasy outlaw. I do believe you're making progress. Since we've run out of time, we'll talk more about this rancher at our next appointment."

Kathryn left his office tied up in knots and got into her Jeep. While she'd been in her session, Jake had left a message on her voice mail asking her to call him as soon as she could. She phoned him on the way back to her condo.

"Jake? Did you get a break in the case?"

"Let's just say your hunch paid off. When that collector in Bozeman gave you a list of serious collectors of Western memorabilia, one of your phone calls to them produced results. A Jonathon Dix from Omaha, Nebraska, phoned me an hour ago asking for you. He's in possession of Colt's gold buckle he bought four months ago off another collector."

The blood pounded in her ears. "You're kidding!" She could hardly breathe. "How does he know if it's authentic?"

"Colt's name is there in gold letters. If you still want to buy it, the price is thirty thousand dollars."

She couldn't hold back her cry of excitement. "Have you told Colt?"

"No. I'm leaving that up to you. This is our first big lead. A word of advice from a man who married a

McFarland? Let him buy his own prize back so he can feel like a man."

Whoa. Her brother-in-law hadn't minced words. She supposed she deserved that reminder.

"Message received." Once she surprised Colt with the news, she'd let him run the show from here on out. *Talk about fun!*

"Good girl. When you get to Omaha, pick that collector's brains. Depending on how long Natalie kept his award and how many collectors have purchased it since, we might be closer to her than we think."

"I pray we are. Love you, Jake."

"Ditto."

It was Friday noon. Without a moment to lose, she chartered a flight to Bozeman, then flew through the condo to pack a bag. On the way to the airport she would arrange for a rental car. No more asking favors from Maggie. Jake was probably sick and tired of that, too.

By quarter to three that afternoon, she drove up to the side of the ranch house. Though it was partly sunny, fresh snow had fallen during the night. She saw tire tracks but no sign of the truck or Xterra.

Not about to be defeated, she drove on to the barn in the distance where she could make out a couple of hands. She drew up to them. They eyed her with male interest as she stepped into fresh snow. The younger one tipped his hat. "Hi! I remember seeing you with the boss at the Westerner."

She nodded. That was last Monday night, but it seemed like a century ago. "Do you know where I might find Colt?"

"Sure. He's at the far pen with the vet. If you keep following this road, you'll come to it."

"Thank you very much."

She got back in the car and drove on. The knowledge that she'd be seeing him in a few minutes was causing her temperature to spike.

"DON'T LOOK NOW, Colt, but there's this knockout golden filly I'd sell my soul for approaching the pen."

"What are you talking about?"

"Turn around and find out, but don't say I didn't warn you."

Colt moved his boot-clad foot off the bottom rung of the fence and looked over his shoulder. When he saw the same vision, he felt a quickening in his blood real enough to convince him he'd just survived a powerful earth tremor.

As Kathryn walked toward him in her cowboy boots, the sight of her blond hair beneath a chocolate-brown cowboy hat blew him away. Neither he nor Tom, who was very married with four children, could tear their eyes from her hourglass figure outfitted in jeans and a dark brown fitted jacket. The fringe swayed with every movement.

"I probably should have phoned you I was coming, but I wanted to surprise you." She sounded a trifle out of breath.

Tom nudged him hard in the back.

"It's a fact you've done that," Colt said in a husky voice. Her hot blue eyes had a vaguely imploring quality that sucked him in. "Kathryn McFarland, meet Dr. Tom Sutton, my vet."

She extended her hand. "How do you, Dr. Sutton."

"I'm doing better than one of Colt's foals."

"Oh, dear."

He chuckled. "But she'll live." Tom turned to Colt. "Call me if you don't see improvement in a couple of days." After winking at him, he gave Kathryn a smile and walked around the pen to his truck, but Colt only had eyes for the stunning female standing in front of him. The urge to carry her off to his secret place on the mountain was so strong, it alarmed him.

"Please forgive me for interrupting, Colt, but this couldn't wait."

He cocked his head. "Don't you know you can always bother me?" His question caused color to creep into her face. It felt like years instead of days since he'd molded her to him while they were dancing. Colt's need for her was so acute, he'd planned to fly to Salt Lake tomorrow because he couldn't stand to be apart from her any longer. "What's happened?"

"Jake called me with some good news this morning. He hasn't found Natalie yet, but one of the collectors I contacted this week phoned him from Omaha. His last name is Dix. Four months ago, he bought your gold buckle from another dealer. It's there if you want to buy it."

She could have phoned him with that news, but she chose to deliver it in person. Now was the time to find out if he was just dreaming this up. "Then I think we ought to fly to Nebraska tomorrow."

To his shock, she didn't give him a reason why she couldn't. Instead she said, "If we're going that soon, we'd better make flight reservations."

So Maggie wouldn't be doing the honors. Another good shock.

"Did you already check into the Silver Spur?"

"No. I came straight here."

Maybe he really was hallucinating, otherwise why wasn't she fighting him? There was a catch here somewhere. "That's good because I wouldn't let you stay in town again. Tomorrow we'll take the twins with us."

At the same time her eyes lit up with emotion, she bit her lip. "Do they know Natalie took it?"

He shook his head. "I told them someone stole it a long time ago."

"They'll be so excited for you."

"That won't even cover it when they find out you're staying over. Follow me back to the house and we'll surprise them."

It seemed the most natural thing in the world to grasp her hand. They walked through the snow in a kind of companionable silence he'd never known with any woman. Before helping her into the rental car, he gave her fingers a squeeze. "I'm glad you came," he whispered.

She avoided his glance. "This was an important find for you."

Colt lowered his head. "I'm glad you came," he repeated forcefully against her lips and felt her body tremble.

"So am I."

What he heard helped him find the strength to shut her door. They had all night after the twins went to bed. Colt could be patient a little longer. Barely.

On the way back to the house, he watched her through

the rearview mirror. It reminded him of the day she'd brought Allie home from Salt Lake. He couldn't take his eyes off her then, either, but at that point in time he was terrified that if he let his guard down for an instant, he would fall irrevocably in love with her.

They reached the house just as the twins were getting out of the Xterra with Noreen. He had the impression that if his daughter's brown eyes opened any wider, they'd pop.

Matt found his voice first. "Katy!"

Their guest walked over and gave them both a hug, backpacks and all.

Allie eyed her father curiously. "Did you know she was coming, Dad?"

"Nope. She surprised me."

Noreen smiled at Kathryn. "Will you be staying for dinner?"

"She's here for the weekend," Colt announced before Kathryn could. "I think steak fajitas sound good. We'll all help." He walked over to pull her suitcase out of the back of the car. More shock because she let him do it.

"How's the bull riding coming, Matt?" she asked as they all went in the back door of the house.

"Dad drove me and Rich over to the Thorntons' ranch this morning. They have practice bulls and an indoor arena. We watched Billy Thornton for a while. He's a year older than I am."

"Is he good?" she queried as Colt helped her off with her jacket. Beneath it she wore a silky brown blouse tucked in at the waist. She removed her hat and put it on the shelf above the pegs. Every move she made captivated him.

Matt laughed. "He's terrible, isn't he, Dad?"

"We're all terrible at first."

"It probably made him nervous with your famous father looking on." They moved down the hall to the family room. Allie led the way.

"Look, Katy. We hung Dad's poster in here."

"So I see. It's what this room needed." She smiled at Allie. "Now it's complete."

Colt's daughter beamed. "I think so, too."

"No, it's not," Matt piped up in a serious tone. Everyone looked at him in surprise. "His gold buckle should be on the mantel. When I told Billy that Dad's got stolen, he acted all weird like he couldn't believe he'd really won it."

Kathryn darted Colt a heart-stopping smile. "How long are you going to keep your children in suspense?"

He studied her enticing features before his gaze swerved to the twins. "We'll have to prove Billy wrong and fly to Omaha in the morning to pick it up."

Matt stared at him with uncomprehending eyes. "What do you mean?"

"I mean someone found it."

After a long silence, Allie turned to Kathryn. "*You* did it."

"I located a collector who knew another collector."

"Oh, Katy!" Colt watched his daughter throw her arms around Kathryn.

"Would that I could find your mother as easily, darling."

An excited yelp came out of Matt, who was oblivious to the emotional byplay going on around him. "Rich has got to hear this!" He plopped down on the couch and pulled out his cell phone.

While Kathryn continued to work her magic on his children, Colt slipped into his den to make online reservations to Nebraska for four people. When he went back to the family room, he discovered the three of them had gone upstairs with her suitcase. He could hear their heightened chatter, the kind that had been missing in his home without a mother.

Colt had tried to do everything for his twins, but he couldn't give them that. As for being a husband to Natalie, how could he have done that when she'd never had any intention of being a wife?

What would it be like to have both?

AFTER DINNER, Kathryn delighted in the videos of the twins taken at different times and seasons of their lives. Now Colt had sent them to bed.

Since she'd arrived at the ranch earlier in the day, it felt as if she'd been playing house. There was a mommy and a daddy and a boy and a girl. The perfect family except for one flaw. The real mommy was missing, just as Kathryn's real mommy had been missing for the first twenty-six years of her life.

How odd that when Kathryn was a young girl on the farm, she fantasized about the people in her make-believe house—her real parents and siblings. She never once saw herself as the mommy, only the child. Then in her fantasies about Considine, she was simply his woman. Kids didn't enter into the picture in her fantasy.

Her childhood was so abnormal, she didn't play like

a normal child, or plan realistically for the future. She never once thought about dating or getting married. Frankly, to belong to a man after her long captivity was anathema to her.

Until Colt.

But he wasn't free. It wasn't just the legality of it. What Natalie had done to him had left emotional scars. How could he honestly ever trust a woman again? There was no violence in him. The shield he'd erected was much more powerful to keep him safe. Today he'd let his guard down a little, but one wrong move on Kathryn's part and the ice around his heart would never melt.

"I'm going to say good-night, too." She started to get up from the couch, but he pulled her onto his lap.

"Not yet. I need this first."

In a lightning move his mouth closed over hers. The hunger of it caused her to gasp. This was no benediction. He didn't pretend to coax a response from her. His blatant longing was unmistakable. They were crossing a line here where fun had been left behind and the real stuff of life was happening.

To deny him now could cause permanent damage. She didn't *want* to deny him anything, but it meant exposing the heart she'd been guarding for years, too. It gave him power to inflict joy and pain in equal or unequal amounts.

"Colt—" she whispered before she gave up the battle and began kissing him back with a passion she hadn't known herself capable of.

He lay down and pulled her on top of him. Kathryn wasn't prepared for the rapture he created. They drank deeply and fully, producing a moan from her. Every kiss sent exquisite sensations through her body. She forgot time and place as his possessive lips roamed her features relentlessly.

"There are no words." He sounded drugged before his mouth devoured hers with barely disguised ferocity.

She couldn't speak, either. To talk meant to interrupt something she never wanted to stop, not even for a second. Between the pleasure of his hands and mouth, she realized a person could die of ecstasy.

Much later, he murmured, "If we were alone in the house, I'd take you to my room."

If they were alone, she'd go with him, unable to help herself. The reminder that Allie or Matt could make an unexpected appearance did what nothing else could. She tore her lips from his and got to her feet, but she staggered. If Colt hadn't been right there to catch her, she would have fallen over.

"It's late," she cried as he crushed her against him, drawing another kiss from her mouth.

"Don't leave me yet."

"You think I want to?"

He buried his face in her hair. "I'm afraid."

"Of what?"

"That I'll wake up and discover this whole day and night have been a dream."

She chuckled. "When I get up in the morning and have to hide swollen lips and the rash on my face from your children, you'll know this was real."

He lifted his dark head and examined her. Using his index finger, he trailed it over her bottom lip. His eyes kindled with light. "You're right. I've left my brand on you."

"Yup. I'm a marked woman." *Colt's woman.* "See you in the morning."

Chapter Nine

"Here's your buckle. I understand it was stolen."

Colt nodded to the owner before hanging back so his twins could crowd around the counter to look at it. Kathryn stood next to them.

The dealer handed it to Matt. "Feel that?"

"Whoa. It weighs a ton."

"More like a pound." The older man smiled at Colt.

Allie took hold of it. "Is it solid gold?"

"No. The base is sterling silver made by Montana Silversmiths."

"Hey, Dad? Did you hear that?"

"Montana's the best."

The collector pointed out the features. "See these ribbons, letters and cast figures?" Allie nodded. "They're made of 24-carat gold. Did you know it took 110 hours to produce this?"

"You're kidding!" his daughter cried in wonder.

"And thousands of hours of practice for your father to win it," Kathryn pointed out.

"I'll make you a deal. I was hoping to sell it for thirty

thousand dollars, but since it's rightly yours, I'll let you buy it back for twenty thousand dollars."

"I appreciate that, but fair is fair." He pulled out his credit card. "If you don't charge me the full amount, I won't buy it."

"Very well, but I won't add on tax." He swiped the card and Colt signed the slip.

"The buckle's yours, Mr. Brenner. Shall I wrap it up in a box?"

"No!" Allie cried. "Put it on your belt, Dad."

"Yeah," Matt seconded.

Colt turned to Kathryn. "You think?"

Her eyes had gone so fiery a blue, they made his water. "Do it."

He undid the one from his belt and snapped in the gold buckle.

Allie grinned. "You look hot, Dad."

"You're the man!" his son exclaimed.

Kathryn sent him a private smile before she turned to the other man. "Will you give me the name of the collector who sold it to you? That person might have other rodeo memorabilia we'd like to buy."

The buckle was stolen property. Colt understood the man's hesitation, but she had a way of allaying his fears.

"Just a minute." He disappeared in the back room of his store.

While he was gone, Kathryn eyed the twins. "Let's show off your dad and take him to that ice cream parlor we passed. The sign said the Cornhusker superduper sundae is supposed to serve six. I would imagine you can finish off what we can't eat," she teased Matt.

In the midst of the joviality, the owner came out with a card he handed to Kathryn. He smiled at Colt. "I'm glad you have your buckle back."

"So am I. Thank you."

"You really have earned it the hard way," Kathryn said when they left the store. "If I were you, I'd always wear it. With it on your person rather than sitting on the mantel or framed against a wall, someone would have to steal it off you and we know that couldn't possibly happen. Don't we, kids?"

"Yup. Dad would annihilate them."

"Is that so?"

"Yes." Allie put her arm through Colt's.

The idea of Kathryn trying to wrestle it away from him filled his mind all the way to the ice cream store.

When they were halfway through their mammoth dessert, Kathryn's cell phone rang. Since yesterday when she'd surprised him at the pen, he'd been in a different world and resented the slightest interference. They had plans to stay over in Omaha tonight.

Whatever the news, she paled and got up from the chair, turning her back to them. Colt felt shredded. The twins' crestfallen expressions said it all.

He joined her and waited until she'd hung up. "What's wrong?"

Her face was a study in pain. "That was Maggie. She said our father slipped on some ice and fell while he was shoveling. Oh, Colt! It knocked him unconscious and he hasn't come out of it yet. Mother's freaking out!"

News of that kind would shake anyone, but this was Kathryn's father, the man she worshipped.

"She's chartered a plane. It's waiting for me at the

airport. I have to go." She looked at him, but he knew she wasn't seeing him. That terrible foreboding he'd experienced twice in his life crept over him once more. Kathryn had ties she could never give up for him. He sensed in his soul she was slipping away from him. It had been a dream, after all.

"Of course. Let's go, kids."

The twins heard what she said and hurried out the door with them. Colt braced her arm as they ran toward the rental car.

KATHRYN FLEW DOWN the hall of North Avenues Hospital to her father's private room. Fearing the worst, she opened the door to discover all her siblings had assembled, yet she sensed at once there was a festive mood with a lot of talking going on.

Her mother sat on the far side of the bed with a happy expression on her face. Kathryn's anxious gaze shot to her father. He was awake!

"Darling girl! Come over here and let me give you a hug."

"Dad!" she cried for joy and hurried to the side of the bed.

"Kind of reminds me of when you were in the hospital and we all walked in to find our Kathryn lying there with your leg in a cast."

"I'll never forget." When she felt his arms go around her shoulders, she started to sob and couldn't stop.

"It's okay, sweetheart. I just took a little longer to wake up, but the scan says everything's fine."

"Thank heaven. If I'd lost you…"

He looked at her mother. "No one's going to lose me

yet. Maggie said you were in Omaha with Mr. Brenner and his family."

She wiped her eyes. "Yes." She felt Jake's gaze on her. "H-he bought back the gold buckle that was stolen from him," she stammered. "When I left him, he was wearing it."

"I'd like to see one of those up close. When are we going to meet him and his twins?"

The family had done a lot of talking. "He has no reason to come to Salt Lake. Right now Jake's trying to find his wife for him." There was no sense hiding anything when they all probably knew everything anyway. She clutched his hand. "What does the doctor say about you?"

"Provided there are no complications, I'll be able to go home in the morning."

"I'll stay with you tonight."

"There's no need for that, honey," her mother spoke. "They'll bring in a cot for me."

Maggie put an arm around Kathryn. "You're coming home with Jake and me tonight. You haven't been over in ages. Robbie's been missing his aunt."

As long as her father was going to be all right, Kathryn needed to be alone, but she refrained from telling Maggie in front of everyone.

She kissed her father once more. "No matter how good you feel, Dad, you look tired. We'd better leave so you can get the rest you need." The nurse in her had come out.

Kathryn went around the bed to kiss her mother. "I'll come to the house tomorrow to help."

"Thank you, honey. We'll love it."

The room slowly emptied. Maggie waited for her at the door to the staircase. "Walk down with me so we can talk in private and not be bombarded by reporters wanting to know about Dad." Kathryn gladly agreed. "If he'd awakened an hour sooner, I wouldn't have called and ruined your trip."

"I'd still rather be here with him until I know he's out of the woods. As for Colt, I get the impression he doesn't take many weekend trips away from the ranch with his children. They had a lot of plans after I left, so the timing was perfect."

"Not for you."

"Don't read more into this than there is, Maggie. I went to Omaha in the hope of picking up a lead on Natalie. The collector gave me the name and number of the person who sold the buckle to him, so the trip wasn't in vain."

They paused on the next landing. "What do you mean 'in vain'?"

"Maggie…he's *married*."

"For heaven sake's, Kathryn. That's something easily dissolved."

"He told me he could've had her declared legally dead a long time ago, but the desire wasn't strong enough to bother. I think he wants to see her again because he's never been able to let go of her memory."

"That sounds sick. Colt Brenner doesn't strike me as a sick man. I think he meant exactly what he said. It would take an exceptional woman for him to get interested in marriage again enough to do something about his marital status. Whether Natalie is located or not, if that special woman comes along, you can bet he'll make sure he's single a second time."

Kathryn hurried down the next flight of stairs. Her sister was faster and blocked her from further movement.

"Stop looking at me like that, Maggie. *I'm* not that special woman."

"There's something you need to know."

When her sister got that look in her eye, Kathryn felt the hairs lift on the back of her neck. "What?"

"This is classified. Jake would kill me if he knew I told you," she admitted.

"That's the last thing you have to worry about. My brother-in-law's so in love with you it's sickening." She walked around Maggie and started down the last set of stairs to the parking level.

"What if I told you Colt told Jake he was going to start proceedings?"

Kathryn almost tripped on the steps and had to grab hold of the railing.

"I thought that might give you something to think about, considering he could still put it off *until* or *if* she's found," Maggie said in a tone of satisfaction.

When they opened the door to the underground garage, Jake was waiting for them. They walked her to her Jeep and helped her in. "We'll see you at home."

"Actually I'm going to the condo. But thanks for the offer, you two. I have a lot of foundation business to catch up on. If I do it tonight, then I'll have time to spend with Mom and Dad tomorrow. Good night."

On the way home she checked her voice mail. Her heart raced when she saw that Colt had left a message.

I phoned Jake a little while ago. He told me your father gained consciousness with no complications and could be going home as early as tomorrow. I can only imagine your joy. If you have a minute tomorrow, call me and give me an update. The twins are very anxious to hear from you.

Colt, Colt. Was it true what Maggie said? She was terrified to believe it, but more terrified not to.

With the phone still in her hand, she realized Donna had also left her a message.

I received a call from Allie Brenner through the foundation hotline. She says it's urgent she get in touch with you. I knew you'd want to know.

Kathryn had just parked in the plaza garage. She briefly closed her eyes. She'd always been completely honest with Colt and honored his wishes, but she couldn't ignore his daughter's plea. Without hesitation, she phoned Donna.

"Hi. I just listened to your message. Did Allie leave her cell phone number?"

"Yes."

"Then will you text her with my number so she can call me direct?" Where Colt was concerned, the need to keep everything aboveboard was paramount.

"Of course. I'll do it right now. I heard about your

father on the news. They said he's gained consciousness. Is he going to be all right?"

"Yes, thank heaven. He'll go home tomorrow."

"That's wonderful news. Talk to you later."

Kathryn hung up and dashed inside the tower. As she walked out of the elevator into her condo, the phone rang. She checked the caller ID and clicked on.

"Hi, Allie."

"I know I'm not supposed to call you, but I couldn't help it," she began before she started to cry.

"It's all right, darling. I'm glad you phoned."

She heard sniffing. "You are?"

"Of course."

"Dad said your father was going to be okay."

"Yes. It's the best news."

"I know you love your father the way I love mine. If anything happened to Dad, I'd want to die."

"Nothing's going to happen to either of our dads, Allie. Mine still has years of living to do yet, and yours is going to see you and Matt grow up, go to college, get married, have children and be a grandpa to them. As Matt says, he's such a dude he'll be showing your sons how to bull ride."

Allie's laughter between the tears was music to her ears.

"What was that frontier museum at the hotel like?"

"I don't know. We're back home. Dad didn't want to stay in Omaha. None of us did without you." Those words melted Kathryn's heart. "Uh-oh. I've got to go."

That meant Colt had walked in on his daughter. Kathryn hung up the phone and removed her coat, reliving the moment when Maggie had called to tell her about their father.

One day they would lose their dad, yet she had the conviction she'd be able to handle it. But when she boarded the plane taking her to Salt Lake and looked back at Colt, a paralyzing chill went through because she knew it would be a different story if he went out of her life.

COLT SAT DOWN at the side of Allie's bed. She'd hidden herself beneath the covers. "I thought I heard you talking to someone. Isn't it rather late for you to be on the phone with friends?"

In a minute she pushed back the quilt and sat up. "I phoned the foundation hotline and left a message for Katy. She called me back. Are you mad at me?"

"No," he said. "Thank you for being honest."

"I know you said her dad was getting better, but I just had to talk to her for a minute."

"I understand."

Her eyes filled with tears. "I love her."

He could hardly swallow. "I'm aware of that."

She drew her knees up to her chest. "Dad? You know that promise you made to find our mom?"

"How could I forget?"

"While you were on the phone with Ed, Matt and I talked about it and we've decided we don't want you to look for her."

Colt hadn't seen that one coming. "Why not?"

"B-because," she stammered, "if she'd been like Katy, she wouldn't have left. I also know you don't want to see her again."

Nope. Natalie had been dead to him since the moment she'd told him she wanted to abort their children.

"Even if you find her, she won't want to see us, otherwise she would have come years ago. We don't want her to come if it isn't her own idea."

His children were growing up so fast, it took his breath away.

She bowed her head. "You know when I was in the hospital?"

"Yes?"

"Katy took care of me the way Mrs. Wagner takes care of Jen when she's sick, only Katy's different and clever and smarter and a lot more exciting and so kind she makes me cry. Oh, Dad, I—I feel so ashamed." Her voice caught.

"What are you talking about?"

Allie unexpectedly threw her arms around his neck and sobbed. Her words came out in spurts. "All those years she didn't have a mother or a father to love her, but Matt and I have always had you. You're the most wonderful father in the whole world."

Colt could hear Kathryn's voice as she'd imitated those exact words of Allie's to him over the phone.

"Will you forgive me for putting you through so much pain?"

He hugged her close. "Allie sweetheart, we've been through this before. There's nothing to forgive."

"Yes, there is. Because of me, you hired Katy's brother-in-law and it has put him and her sister out. Please call him and tell him to stop looking for her. To be honest, I'm afraid he might find her and it will all have been for nothing because Matt and I never want to see her or know her. Matt never really did, but he went along with me."

Well, well...nothing could be any plainer than that.

He kissed the top of her head before letting her go. "I'll call him tonight to let him know."

"Thanks." She wiped the moisture off her face with the sheet.

Colt got up from the bed. He paused at the door to look back at her. "You want to know something?"

"What?"

"If you hadn't gone to Salt Lake and met Kathryn, I wouldn't be wearing my gold buckle. How happy do you think that makes me?"

A smile broke out on her face. "Pretty happy."

"Yup. Good night, honey."

He stopped by Matt's room. His son was on the computer looking up bull-riding trivia. "As far as I can tell, no one's ever had better scores than you, Dad."

"Keep looking. You'll find them." He put a hand on his shoulder. "I was just speaking with your sister. She asked me to call off the search for your mother."

Matt looked up at him. "Yeah. Is that okay with you?"

"It was always okay with me."

He smiled. "That's what I thought."

"Then we're good?" Colt asked.

"Yeah." They high-fived each other. "Dad?" Matt called out as he started to leave the room.

Pausing mid-stride, Colt turned to him. "What is it?"

"It was fun flying to Omaha with Katy. She's awesome."

Awesome didn't begin to cover it.

BESIDES WORRYING about her father, Kathryn spent a restless night waiting for morning to come so she could phone Colt. Her abrupt departure from them in Omaha, coupled with Allie's brief call last night, had left her hanging. She'd hoped to make contact before she had to leave for the Grand America Hotel this morning to give a talk.

At seven, she received a call from her Donna. "I thought I'd phone in case there's anything you need before you take off."

"No. I'm as ready as I'll ever be."

"Good. The Salt Lake County sheriff's chief deputy just phoned for verification that things were lined up on our end. I told him we'd sent our brochures and a video clip to the conference chair a week ago."

"Bless you, Donna. I don't know what I'd do without you. Talk to you later." She hung up and fixed herself a cup of coffee and some toast before getting in the shower. After arranging her hair in a French roll, she phoned her mother. At five to eight, Kathryn could count on her being up.

"Mom? How's Dad this morning?"

"Other than a sore bump on his forehead, he's fine. You know him. He's already eaten breakfast and showered. Now he's dressed and wants to go home."

"I bet you didn't get any sleep."

She laughed. "No, but I didn't mind. They've taken such wonderful care of him, it's a relief."

"I'm glad. Has the doctor been in?"

"Not yet, but when he comes, I'm sure he'll release him. Ben and Cord will be here to drive us home. How soon will you be coming to the house?"

"I have a conference at ten. My part will be over by noon."

"Which one is that?"

"The Great Salt Lake Valley Metropolitan Area Kidnapping Summit. My talk follows the keynote address."

"Now I remember. It's the first one ever to be held in Salt Lake. They're lucky to have you on the program. I know you'll be wonderful!"

"Thanks, Mom. Expect me before one. If there's any different news about Dad, call me no matter what. Love you."

Kathryn had an hour before she needed to leave for the hotel. Though she disliked calling Colt this early, she suspected he was already out on the ranch working. In his message he'd asked her to phone him when she found a minute, so hopefully he wouldn't mind.

To her disappointment it rang several times and went to his voice mail. All she could do was let him know she'd called and would try again later. In a restless mood, she left the kitchen and walked back to her bedroom to get dressed and do her makeup.

With the kind of media coverage this meeting would get, she decided to wear her black wool suit. The tailored two-piece with the long sleeves was simple, yet sophisticated. A strand of pearls with her pearl studs would add the right touch.

While she got ready, she kept her cell next to her in case Colt phoned, but by twenty after nine he still hadn't returned her call. After putting on her closed-toe black pumps, she slipped into her knee-length camel-hair coat and called for a limo.

It didn't take long to reach the hotel. After turning off her phone, she got out and had to face a barrage of photojournalists on her way in to the conference room. Dozens of security people had converged because the governor and one of the state senators had arrived before her. As all of them were friends with her and her family, they got up to give her a quick hug and ask about her dad's accident.

FBI Special Agent Larry Forsythe, the keynote speaker, and other law enforcement dignitaries she knew clustered around her before the meeting started. The room had filled to capacity with local police and federal agents. There were even some CIA. Jake had planned to come, but she hadn't seen him yet.

Once the chief of police had helped her off with her coat, she sat down and tried to collect her thoughts. It was difficult because she kept checking her voice mail to see if Colt had sent her a message yet. So far, nothing.

As soon as the meeting got under way and all the dignitaries were recognized, she put the phone back in her bag and concentrated on Larry's speech. His thoughts echoed the same cry heard from the political arena. He urged local police and federal agents who investigated kidnapping cases to work together and not let bureaucratic red tape slow them down.

In summation, he said, "Utah and Idaho have had arguably the nation's two most high-profile kidnapping cases in half a century. The courageous woman on the stand needs no introduction. Twenty-six years after being kidnapped, she was returned alive to the Senator Reed McFarland family of Salt Lake City.

"May I present Kathryn McFarland, who now runs

the McFarland Foundation, a cause established by her parents in her honor to help fight the terrible crime of kidnapping.

"For the past four years this remarkable, selfless woman has been giving our community everything she possesses in terms of self, time and money to protect our children from suffering her fate. In the coming year she has agreed to be a part of this summit conference as we take it to the western states. She will now address you."

Kathryn rose to her feet accompanied by a thunderous ovation. When it finally quieted down and everyone was seated, she looked out at her audience. "That lasted so long I felt embarrassed *until* I realized something. Your outpouring came from the joy of knowing that law enforcement was triumphant in cracking my particular case, cold though it was for a quarter of a century."

A hush fell over the audience.

"My circumstance and that of my sister-in-law Kit, who was also kidnapped and lost for twenty-six years, were unique. Though today we have the technology in place to catch these godless criminals faster than ever before, it still requires good old-fashioned police work.

"We need more cable news channels that will run whole hour feature programs and get the pictures out there. Our communities have the manpower, but it needs to be harnessed into an army of volunteers who will assist law enforcement in doing house-to-house searches, combing beaches, mountains and forests.

"Unfortunately we have a problem. As Agent Forsythe just warned, we must get rid of the red tape and share every bit of information possible if we're going to do better. To that end you've been given a brochure the foundation puts out. We're trying to work with every hospital, soup kitchen, school, law enforcement agency and media outlet to battle this evil force together. Our goal is to get the citizenry actively involved.

"In view of this, my dear mother and father, who've been the life force of this great cause, have pledged more funds to augment existing law enforcement funds and payrolls already in place in the Salt Lake Valley to fight this war. Together we can win."

She walked back to her seat while the whole room exploded in cheers. Agent Forsythe went back to the podium and waited for the din to subside. "If you'll all make your way to the banquet room, we'll eat lunch while we hear from the governor."

Kathryn put her coat back on and left through the same exit with the other dignitaries. A few yards off she caught sight of Jake and another dark-haired agent, equally tall and well honed, dressed in a charcoal suit and tie. She assumed he was CIA, too, until her gaze lifted to his hard-boned face. Her legs went weak as jelly.

Colt!

"Well done," her brother-in-law whispered, giving her a hug. "Maggie's waiting for me. Your dad just got home. I'll see you at your parents' house later." He disappeared into the crowd, leaving her alone with Colt.

His stare was fiercely intense. "Do you have to attend the lunch here?"

Her heart throbbed in her throat making it hard to

find her voice. "No. My part's done. In fact, I was on my way out. Come with me."

"Kathryn?" Agent Forsythe interrupted. "I'll see you at the conference in St. George on Friday?" She nodded. "Without you, we could never have assembled such a huge crowd. Thank you."

"You're welcome."

As he walked away, Colt cupped her elbow and ushered her out of the hotel past half a dozen journalists with cameras.

"Sorry about that," she said once they were safely inside the limo. She told the driver to take her to her parents' home, then said, "For someone as private as you, this kind of thing must feel like a huge intrusion on your life."

His gaze swept over her features. "You handle it like you don't even see them."

"I've had four years to deal with it. You get used to it."

"The camera has to love you. You look very beautiful today. Cool, like a mountain stream."

So cool she didn't seem touchable to him? What had happened to the man who'd kissed her senseless the other night? Colt sounded so far away just then she shivered.

"Thank you. When you're a public figure, everyone wants a piece of you. It's a facade I've created to distance myself."

"Your speech was inspiring, but then so is your whole life. When I think what you did for Allie, yet she's only one of the many you've helped in the same way."

"Careful, Colt. You're giving me a swelled head."

His sober expression alarmed her. "Not you. You're the antithesis of a narcissist. Someone with a destiny like yours doesn't think of herself."

Why did she get the impression he was backing away from her? What had she done? Pain made her daring. "I see no sign of the Montana rancher today. How come?"

He smiled, but it didn't reach his eyes. "Obviously my facade doesn't ring true."

"Colt?" she cried softly. "What's wrong?"

"Why, nothing."

The tension was palpable. "We're almost to the house. My father said he'd like to meet you and see your gold buckle up close."

"Before I left home this morning, Matt asked if he could wear it to school."

"Did you say yes?" He nodded. "Your son idolizes you. Your daughter, too, but you already know that."

He didn't respond, leaving her more empty than ever.

The limo turned and drove up the winding drive to her parents' Tudor-styled home. It stopped behind the cars parked in the courtyard.

She needed something clarified before they got out. "Why didn't you phone and let me know you were coming?"

"I had to call Jake last night about something important and he suggested I fly to Salt Lake. By the time I made arrangements, it was too late to reach you. He thought I might find the conference of interest. Maggie drove us straight from the airport to the hotel so we wouldn't miss your talk."

"I see." She clasped her hands in a death grip. "Can't you tell me what it is before we go in?"

"I'd prefer to wait until you've seen your father and know he's all right."

His shield had gone back up. Sensing something ominous, she scrambled out of the car before he could come around to help her.

Chapter Ten

An hour later, after a delicious lunch, Kathryn broke in on Colt's conversation with her brother McCord, whom everyone called Cord. The two of them had been talking horses and rodeos, subjects it turned out were close to both their hearts.

She'd put her coat on, looking too gorgeous to be real. "I'm ready to leave when you are."

Cord grinned at her. "What's the hurry?"

Colt didn't give her a chance to answer. "If you'd heard your sister at the kidnapping summit, you would know she has a list of things to do most people couldn't accomplish in a lifetime."

Her brother hugged her. "That's our Kathryn. She's so busy these days, she hasn't even been skiing with me."

"I'm afraid that's my daughter's fault, Cord, but Allie is fully recovered from the flu now and understands Kathryn's attention is needed elsewhere." He shook Cord's hand. "It's been a privilege to meet you and your family."

"The pleasure was all ours, believe me. How soon are you going back to Montana?"

"My flight leaves at five. The twins have plans for us." He looked across the living room at the family seated around Kathryn's parents. Exceptional, gracious people, all of them, but she was definitely the shining star in their family tree. "I'm glad your father is on the mend."

"Thank you. So are we. None of us is ready to lose him yet, especially not his baby girl who wouldn't be able to handle it after only recently finding him. She's his favorite," he teased his sister.

Throughout the conversation there'd been total silence from Kathryn. Colt expected her cheeks would flush at her brother's comment, but the opposite happened. She was acting so different from the warm woman who'd filled his arms the night they'd gone dancing.

Cord walked them to the door. Kathryn hurried outside and got in the limo without waiting for Colt. When he climbed in behind her, she said, "If it's all right with you, I've told the driver to take us to my condo. Whatever you have to tell me, I'd rather talk there."

In less than five minutes they reached the McFarland Plaza and rode the elevator to the penthouse. After they walked into the foyer, she looked over her shoulder. "I'll only be a minute. Make yourself comfortable."

Once she'd vanished, he removed his suit jacket and tie. He walked through the rooms enjoying the sights of the valley from each angle. The fast-moving clouds made for fascinating viewing. When he reached the kitchen, he saw the poster of himself taking up the greater part of her fridge. He'd be a liar if he didn't admit he was flattered.

By the time he'd walked back to the living room,

she'd joined him. Gone were the pearls, the fabulous black suit and cashmere coat, the black high heels. In their place she wore navy sweats and sneakers, but it changed nothing about her.

The energy she brought into a room made everything around her pale. He'd never forget the way she'd kept today's audience spellbound. It wasn't just her looks. It was her spirit, that intangible life force unique to her.

She sat down on one end of the couch, tucking her legs beneath her. "Whatever you had to tell me and Jake must have been important for you to have flown here this morning."

Colt moved closer to her without taking a seat. He put his hands on his hips. "Last night the twins asked me to put a stop to the search for their mother."

Her eyes widened in shock. She shook her head. "Why?"

"I'll quote my daughter the best I can. 'Matt and I have decided we don't want to see her or know her. If she'd been like Katy, she wouldn't have left.'"

Colt had the satisfaction of watching color seep back into her cheeks.

"'Even if you find her, Dad, she won't want to see us, otherwise she would have come years ago. We don't want her to come if it isn't her own idea.'"

Allie had said a lot of other things, too, but Colt chose to keep those to himself.

Kathryn sat straighter. "Your daughter's made a complete turnaround."

He nodded. "She's done a lot of growing up over the past few weeks. Naturally I phoned Jake right away. It wouldn't have been fair to keep him or you on the job another minute."

"My brother-in-law doesn't look at life that way."

"It's because he's crazy about you."

She got to her feet. "Being Maggie's sister helps."

Colt couldn't reach her. "Nevertheless the Brenner family has intruded on the McFarlands' time and generosity long enough. You all have your own busy lives to lead."

"You didn't have to come to Salt Lake to deliver that message."

He took a deep breath. "You didn't need to accompany Allie to the ranch."

Kathryn averted her eyes. "I told you my reasons. Why don't you tell me yours?"

"To thank you in person for what you've done for my kids, especially Allie. Your influence has helped her to resolve a problem that has caused her pain since her first recollections of life. For that I'll be eternally grateful to you."

She shifted her weight. "Whatever small part I played, the real praise goes to you. After I met my father and lived with him, I thought there couldn't be another father in the world to match him. All those years to have gone without, then I was handed the royal prize.

"I was very smug about it. In truth, I felt sorry for everyone else who didn't have him for their parent. Four years went by, then I met Allie. When she told me about you, I realized I wasn't the only person in the world who'd been handed the royal prize. It came as a stunning revelation, believe me. So you see, she was good for me, too."

Colt didn't dare stay to listen to any more. He fastened his tie and slipped on his jacket. "We'll never forget you. Now I'd better get going. I'm supposed to be at the airport an hour and a half before boarding."

She followed him to the foyer. "Have a safe flight home and give the twins my best."

"I'll do that." He stepped into the elevator. "I have no doubts your speech in St. George will have the same electrifying effect on law enforcement there."

KATHRYN WATCHED the door close.

Something horrible had just happened to her world and she didn't understand why. On autopilot she ran into the bedroom for her cell and called Dr. Morrow. She had to leave a message, which meant he was with a patient. "Please call me. This is an emergency!"

With phone still in hand, she rushed over to the bedroom window. It looked out on South Temple. She strained to see if she could see Colt getting into a taxi, but she searched in vain for him. He'd probably used another exit out of the Plaza.

Her body was in so much pain, she couldn't move. When her phone rang, she saw that it was Donna. Though she didn't want to get it, she had to.

"Donna?"

"Hi. Sorry to bother you, but since the conference at least twenty-five calls have come in on the hotline wanting you to phone them back. How shall I handle it?"

Kathryn pressed her head against the glass. "Ask the volunteers to return the calls with the message that I'm temporarily unable to deal with any requests. I'll talk to you later." She hung up, too filled with anguish to function.

What if she drove out to the airport to have a gut talk with Colt? Would he consider it an invasion of his privacy? Disgust him?

Her inner voice screamed yes because Natalie was the only woman who'd ever managed to turn him from a bachelor into a married man and that was sixtee—

A ringing phone interrupted her thoughts. "Dr. Morrow? Thank you for calling me. I have to talk to you."

"My last appointment will be over at ten to five. You come in at five."

"I can't thank you enough."

Kathryn hung up and checked her watch. It was ten to four. The walls were already closing in on her. She had to get out of the condo and made the decision to leave for his office in Olympus Cove now.

Grabbing her red cable-knit cardigan, she rode the elevator down to the car park, not having bothered to change out of her sweats. The trip would only take her twenty minutes. She'd wait in the Jeep until it was time.

On the dot of five, Dr. Morrow opened the door and told her to come in.

"I did what you advised," she said the minute she sat down. "I went to Bozeman on Friday, not only to do business but to have fun. I felt Colt and I were getting closer. In fact I *know* we were, but then today everything changed."

"How?"

"He flew here. I was speaking at a conference and

he slipped in with Jake. Afterward he treated me like an…acquaintance. When he left my condo, he made no overture to see me again. I don't know what I did wrong. I—I think it's over and I can't bear it."

Dr. Morrow sat back in his chair and studied her until she felt like squirming. "You didn't do anything wrong, but you *are* Utah's Joan of Arc celebrity on what appears to be a lifetime mission. Remember our last session. You've been modeling your life after your parents.

"This Colt on the other hand is a born and bred Montana cattle rancher, raising teenagers no less. Try to separate yourself from the facts for a moment. How do you see these two people getting together in a significant relationship? Honestly."

She didn't have to think long about it. "I don't."

He pressed his fingers together. "Neither does Colt. Worse, you're the Anne Frank of our nation who survived. Everyone wants a piece of you. There's the answer to your first question."

Kathryn frowned. "My first?"

"That's right. The second and more important question is, what do you want to do about it?" He removed his glasses and rubbed his eyes. "That's all the time I can give you for now. I'll see you at your regular appointment next week."

COLT SHONE HIS POWER flashlight around the shed. The place was a mess. It had been the catchall since his grandparents had died. Before that, his grandmother had kept everything organized.

He moved between the clutter until he came to the boxes he'd stacked on top of his rodeo stuff. With only five days to go until Christmas, he realized he'd better sort through it if he wanted to give his son a meaningful present.

Allie had been easier to buy for. A private chat with Jen had produced a long list of items his daughter wanted. He'd already taken care of her gifts and those for his sister and her family.

For Noreen and Ed, he'd ordered a Winnebago. They'd always talked about going sightseeing in a camper but never did anything about it. Colt was always encouraging them to take more vacations. Somehow they never did. It was long past time they enjoyed more of life. The camper would provide the incentive and was being delivered Christmas Eve.

As for Matt, he needed something special.

Colt made space in order to set the offending boxes on the floor. In a minute, he pulled a hammer from his hip pocket and pried open the big crate. Using his flashlight he peered inside. It was like finding buried treasure.

"Well, would you look at that," Ed spoke, startling the daylights out of Colt.

His head reared back. "Where did you come from?"

"I was locking up the house when I thought I saw a light coming from the shed, so I came out to investigate. It's after midnight! You sure pick a hell of a time to rummage."

"I only got the idea tonight, but I had to be sure the twins were asleep before I sneaked out. Think he'll like any of this junk?"

Ed snorted. "There's junk, and then there's junk. Are you daft?"

"I was only asking. If I wrap up this stuff, I hope it'll give him some fun opening it. I think I'm ready for Christmas now." He glanced at his foreman. "What about you?"

"Noreen has everything under control. What did you get Kathryn?"

Colt's eyes slid away. "Who in the hell is that?"

"That bad, huh?"

His jaw hardened. "Don't start in, Ed. The twins do enough of it."

"Somebody needs to get to you. Since you flew back from Salt Lake ten days ago, you've been ornerier than Lightning before you broke him in. The hands around here have been forced to keep wide berth. That's something that's never happened before."

Shut up, Ed.

"What did that sensational woman ever do to you except transform your kids and remind you that you were once a great champion?"

"You said it first," Colt snapped. "*Sensational* puts her outside the realm of possibility."

"What are you talking about?"

"You weren't there when she learned that the body the volunteers from the McFarland Foundation found was that of the missing girl. Kathryn has a need to comfort others that goes beyond the normal person's capacity. It's what drives her.

"At that kidnapping conference, she was such an inspiration the FBI has years of speaking engagements and commitments lined up for her all over the West." The veins stood out in Colt's neck. "You didn't see how she reacted when she thought her father might be dying. Hell, Ed, he's her *life!*"

"I hear you, Colt."

He shuddered. "Being kidnapped did things to her I can't fight. You didn't hear her tell Allie how at her age, she swore that if she were ever united with her parents, she'd never leave their sight again."

Silence filled the shed. His outburst left him with nothing but a gnawing hunger that would haunt him to the grave.

"Funny how with all that going on in her life, she left their sight several times to fly to Montana."

"On business for Allie and me!" Colt thundered. "But you haven't seen her pop up around here lately because that business is over."

"If you say so. Why don't I help you take all this junk into my house where it will be hidden? Noreen and I will wrap it for you so Matt doesn't suspect anything."

Colt wheeled around and clasped his best friend on the shoulder. "Thanks for putting up with me."

Ed's expression grew solemn. "You know I'd do anything for you if I could."

"I do. But the truth is, Kathryn McFarland is destined to belong to the world." He looked down at the things in the crate. "Shall we get started?"

KATHRYN WROTE DOWN the number of Colt's ranch house phone before coaching the poor salesgirl on what to say. It was Christmas Eve and all the clerks looked frazzled. But Kathryn had bought enough things to make it worth the college girl's time.

"No matter who answers, just identify yourself and ask for Mrs. Walters. If she's on the phone, tell her just a minute and hand the phone to me. If she's not available, give them your extension number and ask that she phone you back ASAP. Got it?"

The redhead nodded and pressed the digits of the store phone. "Hello. This is Julie at Macy's Gallatin Valley Mall. I need to speak to Mrs. Walters. Oh, good. Just a minute please." She passed the phone to Kathryn, who clutched it in nervous excitement.

"Noreen? It's Kathryn." She heard the woman's slight gasp. "Please don't give me away. Are you alone?"

"For the moment. Colt's sister and family arrived a few minutes ago. We'll be eating at six-thirty."

It was four o'clock now. "Will anyone else be there?"

"Just us."

Perfect.

"I'm in Bozeman and I've brought gifts for everyone, but I want my presence to be a secret for now. When it gets dark, could I come to your house first?"

"I was just going to suggest it. Park around back. I'll leave the door unlocked."

"Bless you."

She handed the phone to the clerk. "Thank you so much. Merry Christmas."

"Merry Christmas to you, too."

Kathryn left the department store with her packages and headed for the rental car. Earlier, after flying into Bozeman on a charter, she'd driven straight to the Silver Spur with her load. Now that her shopping was done, she had to finish wrapping presents.

On the way back to the motel she stopped at a drive-through for a hamburger and fries. She needed fortification for what lay ahead. Since talking to Dr. Morrow, she'd suffered agony hoping Colt would call or fly to Salt Lake to see her. It didn't happen.

Deep down, she knew nothing would happen if she didn't act on her feelings. Maybe nothing would even if she *did* act, but she loved him too desperately not to prove it to him in the only way she knew how.

At six-fifteen, she stepped out of her motel room and felt snowflakes on her nose and eyelashes. Hastened by a gusting wind, the predicted storm had moved in.

By the time she reached the ranch entrance, she could hardly see a foot in front of her. Luckily she'd come here enough that she knew where to drive and anticipated the wide curve up the mountain.

Needing the momentum so she wouldn't get mired, she kept on going when she reached the vale. Ed and Noreen's house stood nestled in a stand of pines near the new ranch house. She could see a glimmer of light and headed in that direction, not daring to stop until she'd driven as close to the back door as possible.

Grateful to have arrived in one piece, she dashed inside the kitchen of the comfortable 1940s vintage home toting two heavy laundry bags. She thanked Noreen silently for leaving the lights on.

Aware that everyone was at the other house enjoying their Christmas Eve dinner, she took a calming breath and undressed down to her underwear. Laying everything aside in a pile, she opened the red laundry bags with their rope drawstrings and started getting into the padded red Santa suit.

The costume was made of beautiful red velvet with white fur trim. She'd bought the full works! It took forever to put everything on, especially the wig and beard, but finally she was ready.

When she went back outside with the two empty bags, more snow had built up on the car. If she couldn't make it over to Colt's house, she would have to call Noreen for help and it would ruin her surprise.

Luckily the ground was level and inch by inch she managed to make progress, but there was no way she'd manage the slight rise around the side of his house. At one point, the car just couldn't go any further, which meant she'd have to use the front door.

That was okay. In fact it was probably better because she could ring the front doorbell. She got this fluttery feeling in her stomach wondering what kind of reaction she'd get from Colt.

Please don't be too angry.

All her gifts were in two big bags. She had to get out of the car and stand there in the snow while she put them into the red laundry bags. The car clock said quarter to eight. Their meal would be over by now.

Once her red hat with its white fur trim was in place, she was ready and started trudging through the snow with her packs. This experience gave her a whole new appreciation for department-store Santas.

The going was slow because she felt clumsy in the big black boots. She'd practiced wearing everything at home, but doing this in a Montana blizzard was something else again.

Kathryn finally reached the front porch and tugged

the bags up the steps to the door. She hesitated for a moment. Maybe it was unlocked. That would be much better. Then she could make her big entrance and really shock everyone.

When she tried the handle and pressed the lever, it gave. More of Noreen's work?

Please understand why I'm doing this, Colt. Please.

With as much stealth as she could muster, she eased her way into the foyer with the bags. She could hear voices coming from the dining room. Someone had arranged a garland around the entry to the living room. The magic of Christmas filled the house.

To her left she saw a beautifully decorated tree standing in front of the tall living-room windows. Beneath it were a ton of presents. The smell of pine and Christmas scented candles filled her nostrils. A nativity scene had been set up on the coffee table. Emotion brought tears to her eyes.

Before she did another thing, she opened the pack and pulled out her cowboy hat. If everything went off the way she hoped, Colt would think Santa was a neighbor. But to give him a hint, she purposely walked over to the staircase and left the calling card of her Stetson on the end of the banister where he wouldn't be able to miss it.

What he wanted to do about it after discovering it would decide her fate. Fearing the worst, she almost lost her nerve. But when she considered what she could gain, she fought off her demons and reached in the pack for the last item to complete her outfit.

Once she'd fastened the belt around her fat belly, she grabbed the necks of the bags with her padded gloves and moved into the living room. Too late to back out now.

Chapter Eleven

"Dad?" Allie cut in on Colt, who'd been talking to Tom. "Listen! That sounds like sleigh bells."

No sooner had his daughter spoken than he heard "Ho! Ho! Ho!" It was coming from the living room.

"It's Santa!" the kids all cried at once.

"I think they're right," Sherry murmured in surprise.

Colt couldn't believe it. His gaze flicked to Ed's, who shook his head in bewilderment. Noreen looked equally stunned.

The kids leaped out of their chairs and ran into the other room with Matt leading the way.

"Merry Christmas! Ho! Ho! Ho!" sounded the booming voice.

Colt brought up the rear in time to see the jolly fat man in red standing in front of the tree pulling out presents from his packs. One of his neighbors had gone to a lot of trouble for this unprecedented visit and looked the personification of Santa. Incredible.

This year, the joy of Christmas wasn't in his soul. Colt wished he weren't so empty inside, but the knowledge that Kathryn could never be a part of his life had darkened his world. He honestly didn't know how he was going to get through it.

"Have you all been good?"

"Yes!" the kids answered.

"Then there's plenty for all!" Santa boomed as he motioned with his arms for the adults to come all the way in. Colt ran a list of all his friends through his mind, but he didn't recognize one of their voices.

When he lumbered over to the children, his body jingled. He handed each one a present. The kid's noisy excitement turned to oohs as they opened their gifts and discovered a large, hand-painted nutcracker.

Amazed by such extravagant generosity, Colt almost forgot to open his gift. It was a chocolate ball arranged in sections and smelled like an orange. He turned to Sherry just as she put a chocolate-covered strawberry in her mouth.

"I'll come back next year if you kids promise to be good!" Santa grabbed his packs and headed for the foyer.

"We will." They followed him to the foyer. "Thanks for the presents, Santa!"

"Ho! Ho! Ho!" Colt heard him call out. "Merry Christmas to all and to all a good night!" When the front door closed, you could still hear his sleigh bells.

Allie came back in to show Colt her splendid-looking nutcracker prince. "I love this! You planned it, didn't you, Dad?"

He shook his head. "I wish I could take the credit."

"That was fun!" Sherry's kids ran to their parents to show them their nutcrackers.

"This is so cool." Matt wandered over to Colt while

he opened and shut the mouth of his mouse king. Colt handed him a wedge of chocolate. "Umm. That's good. I bet it was Roger's dad. He likes to do stuff like that."

"His father isn't that tall," Allie argued. "I've always wanted one of these." She looked at the bottom. "They're made in Germany. Thanks, Dad." She kissed his cheek. "I know you did it."

There was no convincing her otherwise. Colt couldn't imagine who'd played the part—maybe one of the hands—but he knew it was the work of Ed and Noreen. Tomorrow he'd get them to admit it.

He glanced at Sherry. "As long as we're in here already, shall we let the kids open one present before bed?" She nodded. "Who wants to go first?"

Tom suggested they start with the youngest.

"Go on," Colt encouraged Sarah.

While the children took turns, he exchanged a glance with Ed, who was munching happily on chocolate truffles. He held one up. "Mint." So far, he hadn't given anything away.

After the kids opened another gift, Colt went to the kitchen for a plastic bag and came back to the living room to help Noreen clean up.

He found himself counting the minutes until everyone went to bed. Tonight he intended to hibernate in his room and find forgetfulness with some of the Jack Daniels Tom had brought him.

"Dad? Paul and I are going to listen to our new CDs in my room."

Good. "Have fun. We'll see you guys in the morning when more fun stuff begins."

"Yeah." They high-fived each other.

Colt walked over to Allie. "I think it's time you and Sarah went up, too."

"We're going." They gathered up their things.

"Thanks for my nutcracker," Sarah told Colt. "It says on the bottom she's the sugar plum fairy."

Noreen's choice of gift for the kids was a huge hit. Hopefully the new Winnebago would be a hit, too. "Good night, girls."

"Hey, Dad!"

The level of excitement in Matt's voice caused him to turn. His son came running back in the living room sounding out of breath. He was carrying something else in his other hand. The instant Colt saw the chocolate-brown Stetson, everything became crystal clear. His heart gave a resounding clap.

Forgetting everything, he made a dash for the front door and hurried into the snow. It had fallen continually since dinner. His eyes made out faint track marks in the drive. Without a moment to lose, he raced around to his truck and followed them. They led to Ed and Noreen's.

A car had pulled up in the drive, covered in snow. Hardly able to breathe, he jumped out and rushed around to the back door of the house.

"Kathryn?" He charged into the kitchen.

"I've been wondering how long it would take you."

Colt swung around. She was sitting on the counter in a Christmas-red skirt and sweater. Her gorgeous, nylon-clad legs were crossed at the knee. The transformation from Santa back to flesh-and-blood woman wearing high heels left his senses reeling.

"When it seemed like you would never come, I was afraid you didn't want to."

Didn't want to?

"I came the second Matt discovered your hat on his way up to bed." He took a step closer. "I guess you know you turned a regular Christmas Eve into something magical for the kids. They think they're way past believing in miracles. You should have seen Allie's eyes light up at the sight of the nutcracker prince."

"I'm glad. While she was in the hospital, we had long talks. I told her the Ballet West put on the *Nutcracker* every winter and hoped one day she'd be able to see it."

"She loves you, Kathryn. So does Matt."

"I love both your children." Her smile charmed him down to his core. "Tonight I had more fun than you can imagine. I've never played Santa before, but I was afraid in case you resented the intrusion."

He drew in a sharp breath. "You were superb, like you are at everything. I think I might be in the middle of another dream."

She cocked her head, sending the mass of blond silk to one shoulder. "Why do you say that?"

"How long can you stay this time?"

"It depends on this blizzard."

"That's what I thought," he sighed.

"Colt!" Her eyes glinted with pain. "It's impossible to reach you, isn't it?"

His head reared. "What do you mean?"

"Do you honestly think I came all the way here in this storm on the most wonderful night of the year to suddenly take off again? Don't you know I'm here for as long as you want me?"

She couldn't know what she was saying. The muscles in his throat constricted. "No more pretense."

"When did I ever do that?"

"Maybe not, but I need an honest answer from you."

"I've never given you anything else."

Maybe he was cracking from the strain of wanting her so terribly. "It's Christmas. You missed twenty-six of them with your family. Why aren't you home with them tonight?"

"Because I wanted to be here with you."

"Why?"

"You know why! Oh, sometimes you drive me crazy! I love you, Colton Brenner. I'm so madly in love with you it's disgusting."

"Kathryn…"

"You still don't believe me?" she cried.

"It's not that," he murmured. "I saw you speak at that conference. It's clear you're needed by the world to keep other people inspired."

"I'd like to think I'm needed elsewhere. Come here and let me convince you I'd be good for you."

He held back. "I'm afraid to touch you. Tomorrow—the day after tomorrow—you'll have to leave on another noble cause that requires your particular gifts. It's what you do because you're Kathryn McFarland."

"Not anymore."

The blood pounded in his ears. "Say that again?"

She moved off the counter. "That was the old Kathryn who has served her thirty years trying to find out who she really is. Now it's someone else's turn to do that job. Since meeting you, I'm not the same person."

Colt wanted to believe her so much. "Who are you, then?" he whispered.

In the next breath, she wrapped her arms around his chest. "Promise you won't laugh if I tell you something?"

"I swear."

"For quite a while now I've thought of myself as Colt's woman, hiding out on the Cloud Bottom Ranch."

He'd promised not to laugh, but he couldn't help it. Happiness flooded his being.

"I'm tired of being the Lost and Found McFarland. I want to settle down with my own man on our own mountain where nobody knows our business. I want to help you keep raising our children—because that's how I think of Matt and Allie—and hopefully give you another baby. I have such dreams, you can't imagine. If that terrifies you, I'll go away and never bother you again."

Colt crushed her against him. He buried his face in her hair, relishing its fine texture. "How does your family feel about it?"

"Didn't I ever tell you how great they are? They want me to be happy. Imagine that. Of course, they'll be happier if you make an honest woman out of me first."

"You don't have to worry about that. Two days ago I became a single man."

Her head flew back. "You did? You *are?*" He saw heaven in those blue eyes devouring him.

"You don't know the battle I had not to come and get you and drag you away to my secret hideout."

"I want to see it."

"When the snow melts, we'll ride up there. Marry me, Kathryn."

"What do you think I've been trying to tell you? Don't you know you didn't even need to ask? I'm yours for the taking, Colt. I was from the minute I heard your love for Allie over the phone. I've already told you the reason why I accompanied her back here, but it was also because I had to find out if you lived up to the image that had filled my mind."

"I couldn't wait to meet you, either. There was something about you…"

She kissed him all around his mouth without kissing him dead center, driving him crazy. "Tell me about it. All it took was stepping off the plane with your daughter. There was this gorgeous hunk of Western male striding toward me with purpose and that was it. I swear it was like being hit by a bolt of ligh—"

Colt smothered her words, needing her kiss more than he needed air. When he finally lifted his mouth from hers he said, "I love you, Kathryn, but it's going to take all night to even begin to tell you what you mean to me.

"Unfortunately we've left my house full of family who won't be able to settle down for a long winter's nap until we make an appearance. Let's go. The sooner we get this over with, the sooner I can concentrate on you."

He picked her up and carried her to the door. She opened it and they walked out into a white wonderland toward the truck. The snow had stopped falling.

"Oh, Colt! This is the most beautiful place on Earth."

"It is now."

Unable to keep their hands off each other, it took him longer to get her home. "They're back!" he heard Matt shout from the front door as he lifted her out of the truck.

Colt swept her inside the foyer where everyone had gathered. Unwilling to put her down, he couldn't refrain from kissing her in front of them.

"Whoa, Dad!"

He eventually lifted his head and smiled at the family he loved. "I've already got the Christmas present I want. Kathryn has agreed to marry me. It's all settled. Now you don't have to worry about me anymore, Sherry."

His sister had broken down in happy tears.

"Awesome," Matt whispered. His brown eyes had grown suspiciously bright.

"Put me down, darling," Kathryn whispered against his jaw.

As he lowered her, his Allie came running and quietly sobbed as she hugged both of them. "I'm so happy. I've wanted you to be my mom forever."

"I've wanted to belong to all of you forever. Come here, Matt."

While Noreen wiped her eyes, Ed smiled at Colt. "Life doesn't get better than this."

"Nope."

"Who is she?" Sarah asked. She looked as bewildered as Paul.

Their father flashed Colt a broad grin. "Santa Claus. Didn't you guys know Santa's a girl?"

Circle B Ranch, six months later

"Mom? Where are you?"

"In the den, Matt!"

"Good! I need you and Dad to sign this." He hurried in the room and handed her a form.

Kathryn took a look at it. "Did this just come in the mail?" It was the National Junior Bull Riders Association Membership and Release to Ride.

"Yeah. There's some other mail, too, and a postcard from Ed and Noreen. They love the Winnebago. This was sent from Mount Rushmore."

She glanced at it before getting back to the business at hand. "I can see you've filled everything out." It was the parents' consent and release form.

"Yeah." He was so excited he was bouncing with energy. Matt had grown taller since Christmas. His body had filled out more. When he was an adult, he'd be a heartbreaker like his father.

His father. Kathryn's husband. She loved him too much. To wake up in his arms every morning constituted the greatest happiness she'd ever known.

She signed her name. *Kathryn Brenner.* "If you want to get this in the mail by five, then we need to find your dad. Let's drive up to the north forty and look for him."

Colt hadn't known about her doctor's appointment this morning. Now she had news that couldn't wait and she wanted to deliver it in person. Matt's timing was perfect.

"Let's go." She put the letter marked Personal in her pocket for Colt, then grabbed her purse. They left the house through the back door and headed for the new Ford truck Colt had bought her. "You drive."

She tossed Matt the keys. Next month, he'd turn sixteen and would take his driver's test, but she let him drive everywhere on the ranch. He was a good driver; Allie was not as good yet. Under Colt's tutelage he was becoming a pretty good bull rider. Maybe a champion one day like his dad.

"Thanks."

On the way up to the range she phoned Allie. She'd stayed overnight at Michelle's. Kathryn planned to pick her up when she drove Matt into town later. As they climbed higher, she breathed in air perfumed by the wildflowers. The sight of cattle grazing beneath a blue sky made the experience surreal.

Colt was easy to pick out in his black Stetson. He must have seen them coming because he separated himself from the men and galloped toward the truck on Lightning. Like the poster of him, he represented the quintessential cowboy, at home in his element.

They both got out to wait for him. He rode straight up to them. His green gaze bored into hers. "Is everything all right?" Their vigilant protector never took time off worrying about them. That was one of the reasons she loved him with a passion.

"Everything's wonderful." She smiled to reassure him.

"I need you to sign my junior bull-riding release form, Dad."

Kathryn felt her husband's relief. Before he dismounted, she could tell he was trying hard not to laugh.

To his son, this constituted an emergency. Matt handed him the form.

Colt walked over to the truck and signed it against the fender. "You'll need to send the forty-dollar fee."

"I'll write him a check," Kathryn volunteered.

"Here's the money I earned helping Ed." He pulled two twenties from his pocket.

Colt took them and put them in his shirt pocket. "Now you're really official. I'm proud of you."

"If it gets there in time, can we go to Oklahoma's junior rodeo in July?"

"A bargain's a bargain. We'll all go and make a vacation out of it." He gave Matt a bear hug.

"So…" Her husband's eyes traveled to Kathryn. Through veiled lashes he looked her up and down the way he'd done early this morning before they'd made love. Just being near him turned her insides to mush. "Anything I can do for you?"

"I would say you already have."

They were so in tune with each other, Colt picked up on her message and turned to Matt. "Do you mind if I to talk to your mother for a minute?"

"Heck, no. Just don't make it too long," he teased. He walked around the truck and got in behind the wheel.

Colt looked down at her. "Our son's in no doubt how I feel about you. Now talk to me."

"Darling!" She couldn't hold it in any longer. "We're going to have a baby. I hope you meant what you said about having one with me because it's too late to change your mind now."

His eyes blazed with new light before he caught her in

his arms. "Kathryn," he cried softly. "I've been hoping for this since our wedding night. Lately I've worried that maybe something was wrong with me and I couldn't give you the thing you wanted most."

"Oh, I got everything I wanted when I married you. To have your baby is one of those added blessings you hope for but don't always get."

"I wish we weren't standing out in the open where all the hands can see us."

"I know. I picked the worst time to tell you, but as soon as I left the doctor's office this morning, I had to come. I could never keep anything from you. When you get home tonight, we'll celebrate."

"What's that little worry line on your face?"

"I hope the twins will be happy about it."

"How can you even say that when all they do is hint?"

"I know. I'm being paranoid."

His white smile thrilled her. "That's your prerogative as an expectant mother. But I tell you what. I'll bring Chinese home so you don't have to cook. We'll tell the twins together. We'll all want to know everything the doctor said."

"That sounds wonderful. Oh! I brought you a letter marked confidential that might be important." She pulled it out of her back pocket and handed it to him. "Now I'd better go. Matt is already antsy about getting his form in the mail. See you tonight."

He gave her a hungry kiss before helping her into the passenger side of the truck. "Drive safely, son."

Colt waited until the truck disappeared down the slope before he opened the envelope. A small note fell out.

Colt: I sent you this the second it came to my house. I was afraid a phone call would alert Kathryn. Let me know if you want to talk. Jake.

He looked at the letter. It had been typed on paper with a Sahara Hotel, Las Vegas, Nevada, letterhead.

Dear Agent Halsey:
   Re: Natalie Brenner
   Your inquiry prompted an investigation of a cold case concerning the death of a former employee working here sixteen years ago. The DNA sample you sent matched the DNA sample of the estimated twenty-year-old woman hired by the name of Vicky Adams who was found dead in the employees' bathroom on the fourth floor. I've included the Clark County coroner's report with the death certificate. She died from a mixture of alcohol and drugs. No foul play was suspected. The remains are on mortuary rotation.
   If I can be of further assistance, don't hesitate to call.
Office of Internal Affairs

Colt blinked. Natalie was dead.
He bowed his head. Later he would phone Jake to thank him for a masterful investigation. As for Natalie's body, he'd pay for it to be buried at one of the local Las Vegas cemeteries under the name Vicky Adams.

There was no decision to make where the children were concerned. They'd already said they wanted to leave the past in the past. That was what Colt intended to do.

With a new sense of peace that life had come full circle, he mounted Lightning and started down the mountain to find Kathryn. She was his future. Filled with exhilaration that they'd created a new life, he broke into a gallop.

"Hey, Colt!" one of the men called after him, but he was already too far away to answer.

* * * * *

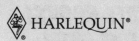

HARLEQUIN®

COMING NEXT MONTH

Available December 7, 2010

#1333 HER CHRISTMAS HERO
Babies & Bachelors USA
Linda Warren

#1334 A COWBOY UNDER THE MISTLETOE
Texas Legacies: The McCabes
Cathy Gillen Thacker

#1335 THE HOLIDAY TRIPLETS
Safe Harbor Medical
Jacqueline Diamond

#1336 THE BULL RIDER'S CHRISTMAS BABY
The Buckhorn Ranch
Laura Marie Altom

REQUEST YOUR FREE BOOKS!
2 FREE NOVELS PLUS 2 FREE GIFTS!

HARLEQUIN®

American Romance®

Love, Home & Happiness!

HARLEQUIN®

A Romance

FOR EVERY MOOD™

Spotlight on
Classic

Quintessential, modern love stories
that are romance at its finest.

See the next page
to enjoy a sneak peek from
the Harlequin® Romance series.

*See below for a sneak peek from our classic
Harlequin® Romance® line.*

Introducing DADDY BY CHRISTMAS by Patricia Thayer.

MIA caught sight of Jarrett when he walked into the open lobby. It was hard not to notice the man. In a charcoal business suit with a crisp white shirt and striped tie covered by a dark trench coat, he looked more Wall Street than small-town Colorado.

Mia couldn't blame him for keeping his distance. He was probably tired of taking care of her.

Besides, why would a man like Jarrett McKane be interested in her? Why would he want to take on a woman expecting a baby? Yet he'd done so many things for her. He'd been there when she'd needed him most. How could she not care about a man like that?

Heart pounding in her ears, she walked up behind him. Jarrett turned to face her. "Did you get enough sleep last night?"

"Yes, thanks to you," she said, wondering if he'd thought about their kiss. Her gaze went to his mouth, then she quickly glanced away. "And thank you for not bringing up my meltdown."

Jarrett couldn't stop looking at Mia. Blue was definitely her color, bringing out the richness of her eyes.

"What meltdown?" he said, trying hard to focus on what she was saying. "You were just exhausted from lack of sleep and worried about your baby."

He couldn't help remembering how, during the night, he'd kept going in to watch her sleep. How strange was that? "I hope you got enough rest."

She nodded. "Plenty. And you're a good neighbor for

coming to my rescue."

He tensed. Neighbor? *What neighbor kisses you like I did?* "That's me, just the full-service landlord," he said, trying to keep the sarcasm out of his voice. He started to leave, but she put her hand on his arm.

"Jarrett, what I meant was you went beyond helping me." Her eyes searched his face. "I've asked far too much of you."

"Did you hear me complain?"

She shook her head. "You should. I feel like I've taken advantage."

"Like I said, I haven't minded."

"And I'm grateful for everything…"

Grasping her hand on his arm, Jarrett leaned forward. The memory of last night's kiss had him aching for another. "I didn't do it for your gratitude, Mia."

Gorgeous tycoon Jarrett McKane has never believed in Christmas—but he can't help being drawn to soon-to-be-mom Mia Saunders! Christmases past were spent alone…and now Jarrett may just have a fairy-tale ending for all his Christmases future!

Available December 2010, only from Harlequin® Romance®.

HREXP1210